Angel of the

A Fantasy for Cat Lovers

L.S. Tucker

PUBLISHED BY: Larry Tucker

L.S. Tucker

Copyright © 2024 All Rights Reserved

No part of this publication may be copied, reproduced in any format, by any means, electronic or otherwise, without prior written consent from the copyright owner and publisher of this book.

This is a work of fiction. Names, characters, places, and incidents either are the product of the author's imagination or are used fictitiously, and any resemblance to actual persons, living or dead, establishments, events, or locales is entirely coincidental.

Edited by: Pam Elise Harris

Dedication

To my wonderful wife, Diana, and my beloved children, April and Steven—thank you for your endless understanding and patience while I worked on this book. Your support and willingness to take on some of my responsibilities made this journey possible.

To my grandson, Joshua, for your invaluable help with marketing.

To my entire family, including my son-in-law Brian, thank you for your unwavering support and belief in me.

And finally, thank you to two feral Siamese cats we call Angel and Skittish, who hang out at the side of our house and provided the personalities of my main characters.

L.S. Tucker

Table of Contents

Introduction 5

CHAPTER ONE: A FERAL LIFE 7

CHAPTER TWO: CYPRESS.................................21

CHAPTER THREE: SKITTISH LEARNS THE TRUTH..............28

CHAPTER FOUR: MILLIE.................................34

CHAPTER FIVE: MILLIE MUST FLEE 41

CHAPTER SIX: PURITY 45

CHAPTER SEVEN: HERETICS IN THE LIVERY 57

CHAPTER EIGHT: CAPTURED 64

CHAPTER NINE: THE ESCAPE 67

CHAPTER TEN: THE TRIAL 77

CHAPTER ELEVEN: THE EXECUTION 84

CHAPTER TWELVE: A NEW BEGINNING 90

CHAPTER THIRTEEN: MILLIE'S NEW HOME 98

CHAPTER FOURTEEN: ANABELLA VISITS.................................103

CHAPTER FIFTEEN: MILLIE RETURNS.................................112

CHAPTER SIXTEEN: ANGEL'S RETURN 119

CHAPTER SEVENTEEN: A CURSE BROKEN 124

Introduction

In a time where superstition and fear reign supreme, two beautiful Siamese cats, Angel and Skittish, navigate a perilous world of medieval intrigue. Residing in a humble suburban neighborhood, they lead a feral life among humans, relying on the kindness of a compassionate family that provides them with food and shelter.

But when Angel and Skittish are summoned back through time by Cypress, a mysterious cat with knowledge of ancient secrets, their lives take an extraordinary turn. They are called upon to save Millie, a kind-hearted healer falsely accused of witchcraft by the manipulative Archbishop Gilebertus. As they journey through the shadows of medieval England, they encounter unexpected allies, confront dangerous enemies, and uncover hidden powers within themselves.

The stakes are high as the cats use their cunning, bravery, and supernatural gifts to outwit human and animal adversaries alike. From eluding animal control officers and vicious neighborhood dogs to facing down the archbishop's guards, Angel and Skittish must rely on their instincts and each other to survive.

As the tension builds, the townspeople begin to question the injustice unfolding before them. The celestial tones produced by the cats during the trial stir a profound sense of doubt and wonder, leading to a dramatic uprising that challenges the very fabric of authority.

"Angel of the Dark Ages" is a tale of courage, loyalty, and the enduring bond between animals and humans. With its rich historical backdrop and compelling characters, this enchanting story will captivate readers and remind them that even in the darkest of times, light can be found in the most unexpected places.

CHAPTER ONE:

A FERAL LIFE

Angel woke first, as usual. Peering out from the kitty tent that the little girl had given them, she saw that the sun had already risen. Her brother, who the girl had, and for good reason, named Skittish, lifted his head and glanced at her.

"It's getting late. Let's get going before the humans come out."

In an ordinary suburban neighborhood somewhere in the United States, two beautiful Siamese cats, Angel and Skittish, led a feral life among the humans. They were fortunate to have found a family that provided them with food and shelter.

"Why do you fear them so much?" asked Angel. "April gives us food. She gave us these warm shelters to sleep in. They almost never come out to bother us. They let us use this small opening in the side of their home. In fact, I wish she would come out more often. I like it when she feeds us because that's when she touches me."

"I don't trust them, Sister," he hissed. "Not a single one. Don't you remember when the big male and that old woman captured us in those cages? I will never go near one of those things again. I don't care how tempting the food they put in them is. Don't you remember how they put us to sleep? Look how they clipped off the tips of our ears! That hurt! They said we were 'fixed,' whatever that means. I don't feel fixed. In fact, I feel broken. Something was taken from us, Sister. Something important."

Angel looked down sadly. "I know. But the girl had nothing to do with that. It was that big male and that white-haired old woman who did it."

Skittish's tail lashed furiously, his ears flattening as he glared at his sister.

"I don't care. I can't believe that you let the girl touch you. She will never touch me. I'll take their food because it's easy. Sure, it tastes better than birds, rodents, or lizards. But I don't like this whole thing. I'm a wild cat. 'Feral,' as they call us. I don't want to have anything to do with any of them."

Angel sighed, memories flooding back.

"I remember all that. But I also remember how when I was small, April saved my life. Remember how I fell into the icy water? You were there. I was struggling to stay afloat. Then, she appeared out of nowhere. She jumped into the unbearably cold water and pulled me out. She held me in her hand and set me on the ground. She let me go. She didn't try to put me in a cage.

"I wanted to thank her then, but she just looked at me. I wanted to be with her to show her my gratitude. I could see that she wanted to be with me too. But instead, she just stood there doing nothing. The bigger humans came running after her, yelling loudly. That scared us both, so we ran. Yet, the look in her eyes has stayed with me ever since."

Siamese cats are known for their inherent warmth and friendliness. But Skittish had vastly different memories. Every encounter involving humans has been filled with fear, pain, and a loss of freedom. He vividly recalled the gloved hand reaching for him and the painful needle piercing his thigh—a memory that was seared into his mind.

He remembered the confusion, the disorientation, and the intense pain when he woke up. Although Angel shared these same memories, Skittish chose to let these particular experiences shape his attitudes and perspective.

"You wanted to *be* with her? What is *wrong* with you? Let's get going. I want to *be* with other cats." Skittish turned and hurried away, leaving Angel behind.

Angel and Skittish were bonded littermates. One was never far away from the other. Their daily routine included patrolling and marking their territory. Skittish would never allow them to become completely dependent on any human.

And so, despite April providing them with food, they were skilled and efficient hunters. Together, they were a formidable team with years of practice, allowing each to read the other's signals with ease.

Their territory centered around a suburban neighborhood near the edge of a large coastal city. The houses were well kept and subject to the strict rules of a homeowner's association. Eleanor Gibb, the association's president, resided at the end of the street, where she could observe everyone's yard with a discerning eye.

Eleanor and her husband Reese maintained an immaculate home. Not a single blade of their synthetic grass was out of place. The pristine exterior reflected Eleanor's personality—meticulous, orderly, and uncompromising.

Eleanor despised the feral cats that lived in the neighborhood, above all, those supported by April's family. She often complained that the cats used her yard as a latrine, leaving their messes on her flawless lawn. She made no secret of this to anyone who would listen.

Eleanor repeatedly called the animal control department, demanding action against the cats. They were often successful, catching and removing many of the offending population. But despite her constant efforts, Angel and Skittish always endured. Their cunning and agility made them exceptionally elusive, much to Eleanor's aggravation.

April's family, compassionate toward all creatures, had given their little-used side patio over to the feral cat population. Each night, it became a haven for the neighborhood's ever diminishing population of stray and feral cats.

Neighborhood cats had their own ways of getting by. As word spread among them, many stopped by for the food April provided. The patio became a place for socializing during nightly activities and a source of nourishment for many. A small but important respite in their otherwise harsh lives. Normally, all the food provided was gone by midnight.

The family's dogs, always intrigued by the activity, were not allowed on the patio or to otherwise disturb the feline sanctuary. This rule ensured that the cats felt safe and secure in their temporary refuge.

And so, Angel and Skittish began their day as usual. Much of their time was spent socializing with other cats. Most were feral, like them. But there were others, a lesser kind of cat in Skittish's view, who lived with humans. They were not real cats. He called them housecats and regarded them with great disdain. Skittish did not socialize with them.

These cats are traitors, he thought. *They lead pampered lives with warm beds trapped inside those strange houses. They must ask to be allowed out. That just fills me with contempt. Worst of all, they smell like humans. They admit to sleeping with them and rubbing themselves all over them. They tell stories of how the humans speak lovingly to them and play with them. That's disgusting. How could they surrender their independence for such a life? To be confined and dependent on a creature so different from us? I pity them for what they have lost. They have traded their souls for security and comfort. They have betrayed their true nature.*

April's friend, Jackie, lived a few houses away. Her cat, Binky, was allowed out while she was at school. As usual, Binky was perched on the block wall, sunning himself as Angel and Skittish passed by.

"Look, there's Binky, the housecat," Skittish said with disgust. "Let's go. I don't want to talk to him."

"You go ahead. I'll catch up."

"Fine. I will be hunting without you over by the tall trees. Don't be long and watch out for the big birds. I'm feeling anxious about them today. I think they may be watching us."

"I will."

Angel approached Binky. "Good morning, Binky."

Angel of the Dark Ages

"Hi, Angel," he said brightly. "Where is Skittish going? I wanted to talk to him."

"Oh, he wanted to start hunting down by the tall trees. We find our first meal there most days."

"He doesn't like me, does he?"

Cats always speak their minds; deceit makes no sense to them.

Angel hesitated for a moment then answered honestly. "No, he doesn't. He thinks you're fat and pampered because you live with humans. He's not fond of them, and he doesn't think we should do that. But I like you."

"Fat?" Binky looked down, puzzled. "Jackie says I'm perfect. She loves and takes care of me. I don't get why he dislikes humans so much."

Angel explained, "He's had a lot of bad experiences with some humans, and it's made him wary of anything associated with them. I kind of like them though, especially April. She feeds us and touches me. But tell me more about your human. I enjoy hearing about them. How is she today?"

"Jackie? Oh, she's great. She leaves for school most mornings, but she always feeds me really good food, plays with me, and hugs me before she goes. I love her so much. Your human April visited us yesterday. We played together in the bedroom like we usually do. April is so nice. She played with me and hugged me. You must really love her."

Angel sighed. "Oh, how nice. But we don't do that. She only touches me when she brings out the food. I tried to get into the house a few times. I wanted to make friends with her, but she stopped me. I think it has something to do with their dogs."

"Yeah, that must be it," Binky agreed, nodding sympathetically. "She always smells like dogs when she comes over."

Angel looked down sadly. "I'm not sure, but I think I smelled something unusual this morning. Maybe a coyote. So be careful. Skittish is waiting for me to hunt for food. I must go now."

Binky's ears perked up with concern. "A coyote? Oh my, I'm going to go home and get inside. Stay safe, Angel."

After Angel spoke to Binky, a strange feeling of unease settled over her. Today felt different. She felt an inexplicable tension. She glanced toward April's house and hoped whatever was coming would not shatter their fragile peace.

When Angel reached the tall trees, Skittish was already there, scanning for any kind of game.

"Did you have a nice talk with Binky?"

"Yes, he is doing well. Jackie takes good care of him. I told him I thought I smelled a coyote, but I'm not sure that's really it. Something is different today, and I just can't figure out what it is."

They found some lizards and mice to tide them over until the evening, when April fed them.

And so, they began their day with something inexplicable troubling them both. This day would be anything but usual.

Angel looked up suddenly, her ears turning toward the sound of approaching barking. She recognized the familiar sound of two of the neighborhood dogs—Bo and Max—both notorious for escaping their yards and causing trouble.

"Bo and Max are out again," she said.

Skittish's fur bristled. "Where?"

"They are running this way through the alley, and I think they have our scent. Quick, through the thicket and up on the block wall."

In a few seconds, they were perched high on the wall. Bo and Max were below barking furiously and leaping up at them. They were getting uncomfortably close.

"What do we do, Sister?" asked Skittish.

Angel's mind raced, searching for experience or intuition that would help. "Look, over by the park. The man with the net and the cages is sitting in his truck. Let's lead them there."

Skittish nodded. Together, they leaped down the other side of the wall into the park. Bo and Max had to detour to the opening thirty yards away, giving Angel and Skittish time to cross the open area to the trees by the playground equipment.

They split up, and Skittish headed to the trees by the play equipment while Angel headed toward the animal control truck. Bo was large and muscular, his powerful legs propelling him quickly around his obstacles and across the open space of the park. By the time Angel reached the truck, Bo had closed the gap between them and managed to sink his teeth into her hind leg. With a desperate twist of her body, Angel wrenched herself free from Bo's jaws, leaving behind some skin and a few tufts of fur. Ignoring the searing pain in her leg, she whirled around to face Bo. Flight did not work this time; she had to fight to survive.

Bo lunged forward again. But this time, Angel was ready. With a powerful leap, she aimed straight for Bo's face, her claws extended, and her fangs bared. She landed on his snout with a furious hiss, digging her claws deep into his flesh. Bo yelped in surprise and pain, shaking his head violently to dislodge her.

Angel held on with all her might, her small but sharp claws leaving deep scratches on Bo's muzzle. She hissed and spat, swiping at his eyes and nose with relentless fury. Her fangs sank into his ear, and she bit down hard, eliciting another pained yelp. Bo, now more desperate than ever, snapped at her, but Angel was too quick. She darted to the side, avoiding his teeth and landing another vicious swipe across his already bloodied face.

The two of them were a blur of motion, a whirlwind of fur and fury. Bo's powerful muscles and larger size gave him strength, but Angel's agility and sheer ferocity balanced the fight. She was a whirlwind of claws and teeth, inflicting as much pain as she could. Bo, usually the dominant predator, found himself on the defensive, trying to fend off the small but fierce cat.

Bo barked furiously, the noise echoing across the park, drawing the attention of anyone nearby. Angel knew she had to end this quickly. Summoning all her strength, she gave one final, powerful swipe, her claws raking across Bo's sensitive nose. The dog howled in agony as the blood spewed, finally breaking his resolve. Angel seized the moment and leaped onto the hood of the animal control truck, her claws scraping against the metal as she scrambled over the windshield and up to the roof.

Bo, disoriented and in pain, jumped and snapped at the air in frustration, but Angel was out of reach. From her vantage point on the roof, she watched him with narrowed eyes, her sides heaving from exertion. She had fought bravely and was safe for the moment.

Meanwhile, the animal control officer emerged from his truck, large net in hand. He saw Bo's agitated state and quickly moved to capture him. Bo was caught off guard as the net descended upon him. He yelped and struggled, but the officer swiftly secured him in a cage.

Angel, still panting from the intense fight, felt a wave of relief wash over her. She had faced a formidable opponent and emerged victorious.

Angel could see that Skittish was trapped in the trees by the play equipment, Max circling below him, barking and snarling. She hurried over, joining Skittish in a nearby tree. They exchanged a quick glance, understanding passing between them. With a nod from Angel, they implemented a practiced tactic.

Angel jumped down from the tree, landing lightly on the ground. She darted past the large dog. Max lunged after her with a furious bark. Angel sprinted away, leading him a short distance before veering toward a nearby tree. Just as Max closed in, Angel leaped back up to the safety of the branches, leaving him snapping at the air.

Skittish then took his turn, descending from the tree with a hiss. He moved swiftly, his body a blur as he ran in the opposite direction. Max, fully engaged in the chase, barked and bounded after him. But Skittish, like Angel, was too quick. He led Max in a wide arc, then doubled back, springing up into a tree just in time.

They continued this strategy, each taking turns to lure Max away and then retreating to safety. Max, frustrated and exhausted, barked incessantly, his attention wholly consumed by the agile cats. His focus was so intense that he failed to notice the animal control officer approaching.

Angel saw the officer approaching and gave a sharp meow to alert Skittish. They both hissed loudly at their pursuer, raising his anger, and watching as the officer crept closer to the unsuspecting Max. The dog, still barking and leaping at the tree, didn't see the net until it was too late. With a swift motion, the officer ensnared Max, securing him before he could react.

Max yelped in surprise, struggling briefly before the officer calmed him and led him toward the truck. Angel and Skittish watched from their perch, their mission accomplished.

The officer placed Max in the truck alongside Bo, ensuring both dogs were secure. He turned back to the trees and saw the shrewd cats. He was called there to capture them, and instead they had turned him to their advantage. Tipping his hat in a gesture of respect, he laughed.

Angel and Skittish had outwitted their pursuers and survived once again.

The clever cats leaped to the ground and sprinted to the safety of their familiar territory. They navigated the maze of yards and fences with practiced ease. They finally came to rest within the clutter of one of their favorite backyards, a sanctuary of overgrown bushes and abandoned garden tools that offered both concealment and comfort.

Skittish, panting heavily, turned to look at Angel and saw the blood running down her hind leg. "You are injured, Sister," he said, his voice a mix of concern and admiration for her bravery.

"Not seriously. It hurts, but I'll be okay."

They settled into a quiet corner, where Skittish tended to Angel's wounds. He licked the blood away gently, his rough tongue cleaning the cuts while Angel winced but remained still. The next few hours were spent in recovery, the two of them nestled together as the adrenaline of their escape slowly ebbed away. Angel's wounds, though not deep, required careful attention. Skittish's gentle ministrations helped to soothe the pain, and Angel allowed herself to relax, grateful for her brother's care.

Despite the excitement of the morning, this wasn't an unusual occurrence. This time, it was the neighborhood dogs. Other times, they had faced more serious threats: the swooping danger of predatory birds, the cunning traps set by humans, and the occasional skirmishes with other feral cats defending their own territories. Each encounter had honed their survival skills, and Angel had come to rely on her keen instincts.

Angel's sense of forewarning grew stronger. It was a feeling she had learned to trust implicitly, a gut instinct that had saved them both on numerous occasions. Today, however, that instinct was flashing red, more intense than ever before. She couldn't shake the feeling that something far more dangerous than dogs or birds was on the horizon.

Angel's mind raced as she tried to decipher the source of her unease. She had never felt such a profound sense of impending danger. It was as if the very air around her was charged with tension, a silent warning that something was coming—something she had never encountered before.

"Skittish," she said, "I can't shake this feeling. Something is coming, something big. We need to be prepared."

Skittish paused in his care of her wounds and looked up. "What do you think it is?" he asked.

"I'm not sure," Angel admitted. "But it's not like anything we've faced before. We need to be vigilant. Trust your instincts, and stay close. We'll face it together."

The two cats huddled closer, drawing strength from each other's presence. But the sense of foreboding grew. Angel's intuition had never led her astray. She knew that whatever lay ahead, they would need all their wits and courage to survive.

Angel of the Dark Ages

CHAPTER TWO:

CYPRESS

Angel's ears perked up. "Brother, something feels strange. Do you get the feeling that we're being watched? I do," she said.

Skittish, her brother nodded in agreement, his eyes narrowing. "You feel it too? I wasn't sure. Yes, something feels off. I thought it was the big birds, but I haven't seen any of them."

Angel's gaze fixed on a black cat observing them from down the street. "Look, Brother. We have a new cat in our territory."

Skittish raised his head quickly, scanning the area. "Where?"

"She's gone now. She was all black, and I just caught a glimpse of her. Look! There she is over there. Do you see her?"

"No. What cat? I don't see anyone."

For the next few hours, the black cat kept appearing to Angel, but Skittish never managed to see her. Just when he started doubting Angel's sightings, the mysterious cat appeared, sitting on the sidewalk and staring directly at them.

"Is that the one you've been seeing, Sister?"

"Yes, that's her. It's like she's following us."

"Well, let's ask her what she wants."

They both walked toward the black cat. As they approached, the mysterious cat calmly stood and moved out of sight behind a parked car. They hurried to the spot where she had been, but when they arrived, she was gone.

"She has vanished again! I'm a little frightened, Brother. Last night, I had a nightmare about a black cat just like that one. It was like she was showing me something scary. I remember there were lots of humans carrying sticks that were on fire, chasing a little girl. It made me afraid."

"Now that you mention it, I dreamed about a black cat last night too, and it wasn't a good dream. I'm beginning to worry that something is about to happen, but I don't know what."

The sightings continued into the evening, but they never managed to catch up with the strange cat.

Darkness fell, and in the dimly lit backyard of one of their favorite houses, even stranger events occurred. Subtle flashes of light danced around them, casting eerie shadows. Mysterious images flickered in their minds, becoming more vivid until they seemed almost real.

"Something strange is about to happen, Brother," Angel said.

"Yes, I feel it too," Skittish replied.

But then, a calm came over Angel. "I'm not scared, though," she said.

"Well, I am. And I'm not sticking around to find out what it is." True to his name, Skittish ran off.

The intensity and frequency of the flashes increased. Finally, after a few minutes, a ball of swirling light appeared. Emerging from the light, a sleek black cat sat calmly before Angel. Her fur was jet black and shiny, lying flat against her body. A distinctive white diamond-shaped spot marked the middle of her chest, and her green eyes glinted with a serene smile.

"Who…who are you?" stammered Angel.

"Don't be afraid, Angel. I am a friend. My human calls me Cypress. In your terms, I am from a long time ago and a long distance away. I was allowed to come here because I need your help with something very important."

Cypress's presence was calming. Angel felt instant recognition and trust. "Was it you we saw vanish? Was it you I saw in my dreams?"

"Yes, that was me. Those events were necessary as a bridge was being built to your time and place. There is much to explain. Come, let us walk while we talk. I would love to see the world as it is in your time. It is all so different."

As they walked, Cypress gazed around in wonder. "What a wonderful place the world has become. Your humans travel around in metal carriages with no horses to pull them. And the houses they live in, so solid but so uniform in appearance. I like it here very much, but my time here is short.

"I come from a time and a place where the humans are very ignorant. They believe in evil and black magic. Some of them have learned how to use this ignorance to make themselves powerful. One of them—a very powerful one—has become jealous of my human. He sees that she is a kind and loving healer, and an especially good one at that. She succeeds when he has failed too many times. Many people have noticed, and they talk openly about her talents. I see his anger and jealousy rising. I have overheard him planning to accuse her of witchcraft. If he succeeds, she will die horribly."

"That is indeed very sad, but what does all of this have to do with me?" Angel asked.

"Your human April and my human Millie share the same soul," Cypress explained. "In a past life, April was Millie. Just as they are connected, so are you and I. We share the same spirit, linked across time."

"No wonder I feel like I know you," Angel murmured.

"Yes, Angel," Cypress replied gently. "We are bound to this human soul, co-travelers through many lives, with countless more awaiting us. Our connection is eternal, and yet the result of our own free will."

Angel felt a profound sense of understanding. "I see now. It all makes perfect sense to me, and it explains so much. But I still don't understand why and how all of this is happening."

"Cats are more spiritually attuned than humans," Cypress said. "The universe has a way of bringing souls together, teaching them, all for the purpose of growth and expansion. Our bond with our humans is part of this cosmic dance, this eternal journey."

Angel took a deep breath, feeling the weight of her newfound knowledge. "I understand now. We are not just bound to our humans but to each other, across time and space. Our purpose is intertwined, and we protect and guide them, as they do for us."

"Exactly," Cypress affirmed. "Love and a shared history bind us as guardians and guides. The Great Cat showed it all to me. You came in intending to be April's companion again, and it was all planned that she would claim you. But this time, she could not. You saw that she wasn't going to do that, so at a higher level, you decided not to stay. And so, you made a series of bad choices. You managed to 'accidentally' fall into the water. You were supposed to return to spirit on that day. But your connection with April was too strong. She knew you were in the pool. From inside her home, she knew something was wrong and that she needed to hurry to the backyard.

"Everything was all set for you to leave. A strong new timeline had already begun. But when she saved your life, it caused a disruption. You are not supposed to be here anymore. You are not happy in this life because you yearn for her so badly. That disruption made this visit possible."

Angel sat silently for a moment while she considered all that was said.

"OK, but I don't understand how I could help you. I'm just a feral cat. What could I possibly do?"

"Are you kidding? You are perfect to help me. You are a survivor. Because you are feral, you have skills I have never developed in my pampered life. You have survived coyotes, owls, dogs, and even humans. You hunt. You hide. You are cunning and patient. When I asked the Great Cat for help, I was told that you were the only one who could help me. I need your skills if Millie is to survive this."

Angel looked down, deep in thought.

"Angel," Cypress continued, "there's more to you than meets the eye. You possess a mysterious power, a strength that lies within you. This gift has been passed down through your spirit from life to life. You and I share this gift, and together we are enormously powerful. Millie needs that power now more than ever. The Great Cat saw your potential and unique abilities. You are more than just a feral cat, Angel, much more.

"If I help you save Millie, will that change my life here so that I can be with April?"

"I cannot guarantee that it will," admitted Cypress. "But it will change many things. It will change enough to make it possible."

Angel felt a profound sense of responsibility and hope. She thought about April and the life they could have together. "If there's even a chance to be with April again, I have to take it," she resolved. "Yes, Cypress, I will help you. Tell me what I need to do."

Cypress smiled. "Return with me to the past. I have a plan."

"OK. Yes, I will go with you."

Skittish revealed himself from behind a nearby car and came running. *"No! No! Don't go! Please! Don't go!"*

CHAPTER THREE:

SKITTISH LEARNS THE TRUTH

Skittish overheard the entire conversation from a safe distance. "Sister, you can't be serious. What if you never return? What about our lives here? What would I do without you?"

Angel gasped, suddenly remembering Skittish. "Oh! Brother, why don't you come with us?"

"Come with you?" Skittish scoffed. "Why should I risk my life for these humans I don't even know?"

"But you do know them, Skittish," Cypress replied calmly.

"No, I don't. I am wild. I am free, and that's how I want to be. I don't pine away for some human that I don't get to *be* with."

"Yes. That is true. It was not your intent to be with your human this time. You wished to move on from this form of cat to another, wilder kind. This was to be your last time as a 'domestic' cat, and your human knew it. You and Angel are co-travelers. You've shared many lives. You are here only because she is. Once she was safely with her human, you were going to leave. You were going to return to the Great Cat to become a larger, wilder kind of cat. Your human knew this. And so, to ensure there would be no chance for you to unite, she decided to be allergic to cats in this life. This is April's mother, Diana."

Angel's eyes opened wide. "Is that why April wouldn't claim me?"

Skittish was appalled. "I have a human? Diana is my human? She's the reason Angel can't be with April?"

"Yes, and it was that decision that caused the disruption. It opened a rip in the timeline. You need to be there to fix the mistake with April's mother. Will you help?"

Skittish sat silently for a moment. "Oh. I had no idea," he said finally. "I'm here on borrowed time anyway, aren't I?"

"You could say that you both are. Your sole purpose was your companionship with Angel, until April claimed her.

Then, you were going to leave anyway. So why not come along too?"

Skittish smiled. "Yes, I will come along. Let's go."

"Good. Then, come with me. There is a particular place where the veil is the thinnest. It is hidden and quiet; perfect for our purposes."

Angel and Skittish followed Cypress quietly to a darkened field surrounded by tall trees. Lights flashed, and everything became still. Before them, an orb of multicolored light appeared. It grew and pulsed with vibrant colors, forming a shimmering, slowly spinning vortex.

Through this magical gateway stood a very tall and imposing figure—the Great Cat itself, glowing radiantly, embodying the spiritual essence of all feline creatures on Earth.

Cypress calmly stepped through the portal. "Follow me."

Angel and Skittish, feeling a rush of wind and a dizzying sense of spinning, followed her. Lights swirled around them as they traveled at incredible speeds. Finally, they stood before the Great Cat, the spiritual essence of all feline creatures on Earth. They were overwhelmed by a feeling of love that they did not want to end.

The Great Cat looked upon his three children with profound love and benevolence.

"You have been chosen for a task of great significance," began the Great Cat, its voice echoing directly in their minds.

"Your journey will be fraught with challenges, but within you lie the skills, strengths, and courage to overcome them. To aid you, I bestow upon you a gift—the ability to see into the hearts of humans. You will discern their true intentions from the colors of their auras, even when their words are untrue, which happens far too often. This ability is both your protection and your weapon in the world you are about to enter. Use this gift wisely, for it will guide you in moments of doubt and danger."

Then, the Great Cat turned specifically to Skittish. "I am sending Angel and Cypress on their mission now, but I would spend a few more moments with you, Skittish."

With a wave of its mighty paw, the Great Cat opened another portal, a pulsating ethereal vortex. "Your journey begins now. Trust in yourselves. Trust in each other."

Angel and Cypress stepped into the vortex, their forms twisting and turning as they traversed the boundary between worlds.

In a township just north of London, they found themselves surrounded by the sights and sounds of medieval England when they emerged. The town's bustling market, rustic homes, and lush countryside stood in sharp contrast to the modern world they had just left.

Skittish sat alone with the Great Cat. The majestic feline gazed at him with an expression of deep fondness.

"What a wonderful cat you are, Skittish," the Great Cat stated, its voice resonating with warmth. "Our time together has truly been enriching. You have shown remarkable growth, and your journey has also allowed me to expand my understanding and connection with all my feline children. There is a new adventure waiting for you once this one is over. It's a path you chose before you were born into this life. To no longer be a 'puny domestic cat,' as you put it. You have decided to become a 'higher cat.' And because of free will, so shall it be. You are to be one of my largest and most powerful, living in a wild, exciting place called Africa.

"You have chosen an arduous life. It will be a life filled with challenges of all kinds. You will face the raw forces of nature, compete with fellow creatures, and navigate the vast, untamed landscapes. Your first few attempts may end quickly. But with each try, you will learn. Each day will demand strength, agility, and wisdom. Eventually, you will exist to your fullest potential. Each life is precious. Therefore, enjoy this life that you have. Enjoy it to the fullest, for there will be times that you yearn for its ease, connections, and joys."

With those final words echoing in his ears, Skittish felt a surge of readiness and purpose. He learned that he was the creator of his destiny. With a nod, Skittish absorbed the vision of his future life, a mixture of awe and resolve welling within him.

"Go now and join Angel and Cypress on this great quest."

With that, the Great Cat waved its paw, sending Skittish spinning through the fabric of time and space. Moments later, lights flashed, and a new vortex appeared. Skittish stepped out and looked around.

"This place is so different from our home," he noted, wrinkling his nose. "The scents here are offensive, and the houses are so strange."

"You will get used to it," Cypress commented. "Come, follow me. There is much to learn, and you must try to stay out of sight. The dangers here are unlike those you have known."

With their new sight, and Cypress's guidance, they began to navigate this ancient world. They were on a mission to save Millie as they made their way into the heart of the township. Angel and Skittish were participants in a quest that spanned the ages.

CHAPTER FOUR:

MILLIE

With Cypress in the lead, staying in the shadows and moving quickly and quietly from hiding place to hiding place, Angel and Skittish followed a woman through the marketplace. She moved with a grace and kindness that brightened the dreary surroundings—a beacon of hope in a time of suspicion and fear.

This was Millie, the healer, whose spirit resonated deeply with that of April.

Angel observed Millie with great wonder. "I see the woman you call Millie, but I also see April. Their inner most colors are identical."

"Yes, they are. Humans can't see the glowing colors like we do. It's part of their nature. Though it makes little sense to us, they chose this."

They watched Millie shop. She was treated with great respect by everyone she met. They all greeted her warmly. People approached her to thank her for past healings, often gifting her produce and goods she would otherwise have paid for.

The three cats watched from their hiding place as a beautiful young girl approached Millie.

"That one is called Abigale," said Cypress. "She is the main reason Millie is in danger."

"How can that be?" asked Angel.

"Millie helped her where another could not. This includes the powerful, evil man I told you about. Millie's ability to help has cast doubt on his power over these people. He's very angry about it." With a tilt of her head, Cypress directed her gaze across the square. "Look at the man staring at them. Notice his energy."

Angel studied the man intently. "I have always seen the colors of their energy, but with our gift of extra sight, I now see and understand them so much better. This is very disturbing. I see that he is jealous of Millie. He is almost blind with rage. It's about the things people are saying about him because of something she did. Who is he?"

"He goes by the name Archbishop Gilebertus and is well known. He holds a position of significant authority within the organization they refer to as the church. My Millie holds the church in great regard. She goes there often to talk to God. She considers it the only intermediary between the Creator and the people. She considers the clergy to be the gatekeepers to heaven. She holds them in great respect. They run hospitals and provide for the poor, widows, and orphans. They guide their followers toward a deeper understanding of the Creator. However, this man, Gilebertus, is corrupt. He has strayed far from the path he vowed to follow. He wields his authority without regard for the spiritual damage he causes. Now, look at Abigale and Millie. Can you tell what they are expressing to each other?"

Angel turned her gaze to Abigale. "Yes! Yes, I can. I understand perfectly. Abigale is expressing gratitude, as she has many times, for Millie's help to have children. She will give birth to her first child soon, and all is going well. How did this come about, Cypress?"

"Abigale believed she was barren. She turned to their church and spent many hours praying for a child. That man you see, Archbishop Gilebertus, after years of unanswered prayers, declared it was God's will that she remained barren. Word of this spread. This was a source of great shame for her and her family. They were the object of much negative talk. She might have even lost her mate. Sometime later, she crossed paths with

Millie here in the marketplace. She talked about her sorrow and later visited Millie at her home. I was there. I saw the discoloration in Abigale's energy that resonated with one of Millie's herbs. I signaled for her to use it. About three months later, there was great excitement. Abigale was with child. The entire town knew about it, and it led to much ridicule of the archbishop. Similar things had happened before. He lost some of his influence that day, and it angered him greatly. That is the hatred you see in his colors. I overheard him plotting against her. He plans to accuse her of witchcraft, which, in this time and place, is a death sentence. It is up to us to find a way to save her."

Angel gave Cypress a sideways glance. "Did you say you have a plan?"

"Well, yes, I do, kind of. We will have to rely on our new sight. And we also have an ally."

"A human?" asked Skittish.

"Yes, you will meet him soon. He is not part of the church, but he is highly educated and spiritual. He embodies all that the archbishop claims to be but is not. His name is Friar Rufus. He visits Millie often, is pure of heart, and loves her dearly. He is due to visit her this evening. Before he arrives, I should tell you more about Millie. She is a healer. She has her own significant gifts. And because she has learned how to listen to me, we have healed many, so much so that she is known beyond this township. People have begun seeking her out for healing."

"That sounds very positive," said Angel.

"It should be, but remember what I said about those who use ignorance and fear to empower themselves?"

Angel and Skittish nodded.

"Well, someone like Millie, who is so in tune with herself and us cats, poses a threat to their power. Some in the church, who are like the archbishop, dislike it when anyone disproves their dominion over them. It diminishes their control and thus, their power. This, more than anything, cannot be tolerated. I can see that Millie is finishing up her shopping. She will be leaving the marketplace soon. Come, let's follow her."

They followed her to a modest but welcoming cottage on the outskirts of the township. Millie had noticed her feline followers.

"Pray tell, whom do we behold?" Millie smiled, looking at the two Siamese cats. "By my troth, never have mine eyes beheld such curious mousers. Thou art fair to look upon, yet what peculiar colors thou dost wear."

All three cats exchanged glances.

"Did you see that color change?" asked Cypress. "Do you know what that meant?"

Of course, they did. From Millie's reaction, they immediately understood that Siamese cats were unknown in this time and place, making their presence particularly conspicuous.

"Yes, that was fear," said Skittish. "A human feared me. Even though for only a short time, I kind of liked it."

"This is no time for such things, Skittish," said Cypress. "This is a problem. We need to be as inconspicuous as possible. Any human who sees you will react similarly, if not worse. You will have to stay in the shadows. Never let a human see you if you can help it."

Skittish acknowledged the gravity of the situation. "Understood," he said, his voice more subdued. "I will stay hidden."

"What about Friar Rufus?" asked Angel. "Do we let him see us?"

Cypress sat silently. It was indeed a good question. She was planning on his help. She remembered things the Great Cat had told her. How attitudes were changing. Humans were growing in their hearts. They were tired of the persecution of innocents. They no longer derived pleasure from the spectacle of the witch trials. Many were complaining among themselves about it. Many were openly questioning whether these trials were right.

Cypress knew Friar Rufus well and soon decided they could trust him. "I can see from his colors that he is a good man. His entire life has centered around his wish to give and be of service. He has vowed to remain poor and humble. I have noticed that he will go against the teachings of the church if he sees that they do not ring true. He knows right from wrong, which is rare for a human in these times. I think we must trust him. But let me introduce you. I will signal Millie to help me."

Meanwhile, Millie was fascinated by the two uniquely colored cats.

"So fair, so beautiful! I'll wager thee art hungry," she said sweetly.

Reaching into her basket, she pulled out the large fish she had just been gifted in the marketplace and proceeded to cut off several large pieces. Cypress immediately took it.

"Hither thou art your portion, fair beast," she said, offering a piece to Angel. Angel trusted her immediately and accepted it.

Skittish, however, remained cautious. His nature had always been to avoid getting too close to humans. Now he struggled with new feelings. Understanding her intent made him want to accept the food, but his old impulses were strong.

Slowly, he approached as his new sight overcame his trust issues. He could see her intent was pure. He could see her love. Finally, slowly, he walked up to Millie and accepted the fish. This was a huge step for Skittish. Never had he allowed himself to approach a human.

Something amazing happened then. Despite himself, his affectionate nature overcame him. Arching his back, he rubbed his side against Millie's leg, back and forth. Then, as he allowed Millie to pet him, he felt his first loving human touch.

CHAPTER FIVE:

MILLIE MUST FLEE

A short time later, they heard a knock at the door. It was Friar Rufus. Skittish and Angel quickly found hiding places.

"Come in, Rufus," said Millie.

"Good day, sweet Millie. Are you well this glorious day?" asked Friar Rufus as he entered.

"Indeed, I am healthy, good friar. Please be seated and share tea with me," said Millie.

"Bless you, Millie. I will have tea with you, but I do not bring glad tidings."

Friar Rufus lowered his head and spoke firmly with earnest. "This evening, a convocation of the church's holy order was held. Archbishop Gilebertus summoned Mayor Marcus and the priests of the abbey for a grave council. He spoke of heretics who consort with the devil to undermine the church. He had a scroll bearing the names of those who must be watched most suspiciously. The good mayor, at great peril, entrusted me with the names on the scroll. Your name was inscribed upon that list."

Millie gasped. "Nay! Such tidings cannot be true! I am a devout and loyal believer. I adhere to the church's teachings with unwavering regularity. I attend every Sunday mass as behooves all good Christians."

From their hiding place, Cypress turned to Angel and Skittish. "I don't understand most of their words, but I can tell that something drastic has happened. Millie must have found out that her loving and healing nature has angered the powerful man. See her colors changing?"

"Yes, I see fear in both of them," said Angel. "She is hurt in her heart. What do we do now? Do we reveal ourselves to him like we planned?"

Cypress sighed. "Yes. We do. She needed to know, and now she does. This is a good thing. It is time to introduce you to Friar Rufus. Let's go."

Cypress walked out from the shadows, followed closely by Angel and Skittish.

"Follow my lead," Cypress said as she began nodding her head and pacing in small circles. "This is how she knows when I am trying to guide her. She pays careful attention to me when I do this. We have healed many this way."

With that, Cypress walked to the space between Millie and Friar Rufus. She began her communication demeanor and motions. Millie recognized it. Cypress held her tail in a certain position as she kneaded the floor. Then, she looked at Millie and blinked slowly twice. Following Cypress's lead, Angel and Skittish mimicked her movements. It lasted only a few moments, but it was enough.

Millie gasped. "Those motions made by Cypress are the very ones she employs when aiding me in healing. These cats are trying to convey a message to me."

Rufus stopped and stared at the cats. "Good heavens, what curious cats these are. Pray, Millie, what manner of mousers are these? Never have I seen such peculiar markings. They are quite fair to look upon but so wondrously strange."

"Verily, they appeared with Cypress but a moment ago," said Millie. "Indeed, they are a most uncommon hue. But they seem very kind. I think Cypress brought them here to meet me. She seems to be trying to signal me about something important. Though its nature eludes me."

"The cats are most interesting, Millie, but let us not stray from the heavier matter. The archbishop was most adamant. His eyes are upon you with great scrutiny. The mayor was, in fact, tasked to recount to him your doings. He was forced to confess that he had seen a black cat in your care. Such creatures are often deemed to be familiars of witchery. I would counsel you to contemplate a swift departure from this township, lest you face trial for witchcraft."

"Alas, good friar," Millie lamented. "My entire life has been within this hamlet. Where shall I go? I have no living kin. I alone survived childhood's cruel afflictions."

Millie cried. Friar Rufus offered his shoulder and wept with her.

"Yield not to despair, dear Millie," he said. "A solution yet veiled shall present itself. Trust in the Lord's bounty. Believe in His providence. He could not forsake one such as you. My faith is steadfast. For a time, you are shielded. Even an archbishop must bring forth evidence, however contrived, to lend weight to his charges. This may well draw long. Perchance sufficient respite to convey you to sanctuary."

"Thy words give me solace, kind friar. I pray they hold truth."

"You are held dear by all, good Millie. I have spread the word to gather a cadre of steadfast companions to meet me at the stables. You have brought healing to many of their ailments. Each soul in this township bears witness to your benevolence, recounting how you delivered them or their kin from affliction. Pray, gather your essentials for a life anew elsewhere."

Suffering in great despair, she gathered her most precious belongings, ready to flee the only home she had ever known.

CHAPTER SIX:

PURITY

Concealed by the darkness, Cypress, Angel, and Skittish made their way through the secret passageways that wound throughout the township. These routes were known only to the cats, dogs, rats, and other small mammals who lived below the awareness of humans. They finally arrived at a small opening leading to the lower levels of the abbey.

"Follow me; I know the way. We have a friend here. His name is Purity. He knows the archbishop well," Cypress said.

Ensuring they made no noise and stayed out of sight, they navigated the bustling kitchen, past praying priests, parishioners, and guards patrolling the corridors, until they reached a plush bedroom. Inside, they came face-to-face with a large, pure white cat whose calm and relaxed manner spoke of his wisdom and experience.

"Greetings, Cypress. Who are your strangely marked friends?" Purity asked.

"Their humans call them Angel and Skittish. With the help of the Great Cat, they have crossed great distances of time and space to complete an important mission. We need your help," Cypress explained.

"This is indeed a great moment. Not many have been so blessed to be called by the Great Cat. How can I assist you?"

"You told me how your powerful human has very bad feelings and intentions toward my human, Millie. The Great Cat helped me summon Angel and Skittish to help me save her. We hope you can help us."

Purity let out a sigh, his tone heavy with sadness. "It wasn't always this way with him. He was once humble, genuinely devoted to his faith. Unfortunately, his mentors have been cynical and corrupted by greed.

"He used to glow with wonderful intentions to serve his fellow humans. But now his colors have turned dark and murky. I've tried to guide him back, but he ignores my messages. The only thing he seems to love is his power and me. He was trained by the church to suspect cats of consorting with evil. But because I am pure white, he believes that cannot be true of me. However, he views black cats differently. You must try to never let him see you, Cypress. And never allow him to capture you. I still love him, but I've given up hope of returning him to his original vision. I will help in any way I can though. Do you have a plan?"

"The Great Cat has endowed the three of us with a special gift. We can see and understand human intentions clearly. If you can inform us of the archbishop's activities, we might be able to warn our humans to escape."

"I will tell you as quickly as I can when I see them beginning to act against Millie."

"Thank you, Purity. We need all the help we can get."

At that moment, the archbishop walked by with Mayor Marcus.

"I must go," said Purity. "I am expected to be with him during these times."

Cypress turned to Angel and Skittish. "Angel, I need your skills and your sight. That was Mayor Marcus with the archbishop. They likely will be discussing Millie. We need to know what transpires between them. It's too risky for all of us, especially me, to attend. See if you can make your way into this meeting."

Angel followed the two men into a meeting chamber deep within the abbey, sneaking in behind them undetected and hiding in the shadows. Gilebertus gestured for Marcus to take a seat at an ornate table. The archbishop moved with deliberate calm, pouring two glasses of red wine from a silver decanter.

He handed one to Marcus and then eased into his own high-backed chair, an easy smile playing on his lips.

Purity leapt gracefully into his lap, curling up with a soft purr. Gilebertus's smile broadened as he stroked Purity's fur, the gentle motions contrasting sharply with the intensity of the meeting's purpose. Angel, crouched beneath a nearby chair, could see both men clearly. Their auras glowed with an intensity that revealed their inner turmoil. Marcus's colors were a swirl of confusion and unease, while Gilebertus's aura pulsed with a dark, manipulative energy. Angel listened intently. Even though she did not understand the words, she picked up the intent of every subtle shift in tone.

"Mayor Marcus, it is imperative that thou provide the constables to apprehend Millie. She is a witch, a consort of the devil, and it is our duty to cleanse our town of her malevolent influence."

Angel could see Marcus's glowing colors were a turbulent mix of angry reds and stressed purples, swirling around him like a storm. His jaw was clenched tight, the muscles in his face and neck visibly taut with tension. The weight of the decision he was being forced to make was profound. Angel felt a pang of empathy for him, sensing the moral struggle he faced.

"Your Grace, I hold great reverence for the church's authority, yet I cannot, in good conscience, apprehend Millie. She hath saved my son's life with her healing arts. I find it hard to believe that a servant of the devil could possess such compassion."

"Did not thy son seek solace within the church, Mayor? Did we not beseech the Lord for his recovery? Just because his healing did not transpire forthwith doth not necessarily imply that Millie was his savior. Divine intervention worketh in mysterious ways."

Marcus stood and paced behind his chair, his steps quick and restless. He took a deep drink of his wine, as if trying to find courage or calm in the liquid. Turning sharply, he faced the archbishop, his eyes burning with a mixture of defiance and resignation.

"But thy prayers bore no fruit, and Millie's remedies did. She tended to him day and night, and mine own eyes witnessed his improvement. Canst thou so readily dismiss her role in his recovery?"

Still smiling, Gilebertus answered calmly, his voice smooth and untroubled. His hand continued to move in easy, loving strokes, petting Purity with a gentle rhythm. The contrast between his serene demeanor and Marcus's agitation was clear. Gilebertus's eyes never wavered, maintaining their steady, almost soothing gaze. He seemed to radiate an air of unshakeable confidence; his smile unwavering as he spoke. The calmness in his voice was almost hypnotic, each word carefully measured, designed to disarm and persuade.

"Thou art a man of faith, Marcus. Surely, thou comprehendest that the devil can cloak his deeds as acts of benevolence to deceive us. Millie may have easily woven a spell to feign her healing, or perchance he recovered of his own accord. How canst thou be certain?"

The mayor paced again, his steps echoing in the chamber. Then, with a determined glint in his eye, he leaned toward Gilebertus, placing both hands firmly on the table.

"I know what mine eyes beheld. I witnessed a woman wholly devoted to healing, not one consorting with dark forces. And my son's recovery was too precise, too directly linked to her ministrations, to be mere happenstance."

Gilebertus stopped petting Purity and stared at the mayor for a long moment. The smile vanished from his face, replaced by a stern, unyielding expression. His voice turned terse and commanding.

"The church, Mayor Marcus, stands as the ultimate arbiter of those who consort with the devil, not the local governance. Thou must defer to our judgment in matters of spiritual and moral peril. How dost thou know that she did not afflict thy Robbie with sickness, only to feign his healing thereafter? It is not thy place to question our findings."

Marcus paced once more, running his fingers through his hair. He then turned sharply to face the archbishop. "I harbor no desire to defy the church, Your Grace, yet I cannot ignore the dictates of mine own conscience. Apprehending Millie would be a grievous injustice. She is a healer, not a witch. The townsfolk esteem her, and they shall not easily comprehend this arrest. It may bring more harm than good."

Gilebertus retorted, his tone terse and threatening, each word carrying an unmistakable edge, "Thou dost risk the church's wrath, Marcus. Yea, thou dost imperil the very soul of our town. If thou dost not act, thou shalt be complicit in her wicked deeds. Dost thou desire that burden upon thy conscience?"

Marcus sat back down at the table and took another drink of his wine. He tilted his head and clenched his jaw. Angel observed Marcus intently, the swirling colors around him revealing a silent tale. He was grappling desperately to reconcile his deep sense of justice with the harsh, unyielding reality of the situation. His mind was a maelstrom of conflict as he sought a path that would uphold his values and integrity without compromise.

"I seek to safeguard my people from true harm, not from fancied threats. I shall not apprehend Millie sans clear proof of her transgressions. If thou hast evidence, present it. I shall not act upon fear and suspicion alone."

Gilebertus placed Purity gently on the floor and stood. He was a tall and imposing figure. He continued in a commanding voice, leaving no doubt of his seriousness. His posture was rigid, and his eyes bore into Marcus with an intensity that seemed to pierce through to his very soul.

"Thou dost leave me no recourse, Mayor. I shall find another path to ensure Millie faces justice. And take heed, thy reluctance shall not fade from memory."

Marcus stood, facing Gilebertus squarely.

"And I shall not forget the church's readiness to condemn an innocent woman. If justice thou dost seek, Your Grace, seek it with truth, not with guile."

The archbishop composed himself somewhat. Taking a deep breath, he softened his tone and demeanor, hoping to appeal to Marcus's sense of duty and reason.

"Mayor Marcus, I comprehendest thy reluctance. Yet thou must perceive reason. The church wields arts and lore surpassing the ken of common folk. Place thy faith in our sagacity. And provoke me not, good mayor, lest thy future in the service of thine office be imperiled."

Marcus took a great pause at these words, standing silently for several moments. Angel again saw and understood the whirl of colors in his aura. The weight of the decision bore heavily upon him. His future was at stake. If he defied the archbishop, he risked losing everything he had worked for. Yet, if he complied, he would betray a woman who had shown nothing but kindness and healing to his community. He took a deep breath, the archbishop's threat echoed in his ears, reminding him of the power the church held over his future. His hands clenched at his sides, knuckles whitening as he fought the inner turmoil.

Finally, with great anguish, he replied, his voice heavy with sorrow and resignation. "Verily, Your Grace. I shall muster the constables. But be it known: I act thus under compulsion and with a heart burdened. I pray that thou art not mistaken concerning Millie."

"Thy cooperation is duly acknowledged, Mayor. Thou hast chosen wisely. The hamlet shall know greater safety by this deed."

Angel returned to Cypress and Skittish. "The mayor is reluctant and conflicted but has agreed to cooperate with the archbishop. They will be taking action soon."

"We need to act quickly," said Cypress. "Let's follow the mayor."

They mayor stopped by the main police station and remained inside for several minutes. Finally, he emerged. His sad and troubled colors betrayed what had happened inside. Their time was short. From there, he proceeded straight home. Ensuring they stayed hidden, the cats peered through a window. Cypress saw Anabella, the mayor's wife.

"I need to get to Anabella. I know her well, and I think she can help us," said Cypress. Unfortunately, a large dog was in the room with her. "Skittish, can you distract their dog?"

"Of course," said Skittish. "Leave him to me."

Skittish emitted a high-pitched screech, inaudible to humans but clear to the dog, who immediately ran to the window, barking. Skittish remained hidden, frustrating the dog, who wouldn't stop barking despite the mayor's attempts to quiet him. Finally, the mayor, annoyed, led the dog out to his kennel.

"There," he said, irritated. Upon returning, he asked for his pipe and sat down.

Anabella was very upset. "Thou wilt not suffer them to apprehend Millie, wilt thou?"

"Thou knowest well that I discuss not matters of city governance with thee, my dear. It is a matter of principle to me. I find it hard to believe that Millie is a witch, yet the archbishop speaks with such conviction. And what know I of these high matters better than he?"

Anabella stamped her foot in frustration. "This virtuous woman hath saved our son's life! Recallest thou not how she watched over him the live-long night, applying poultices to his breast and back? Hast thou forgotten the draughts she brewed for his ailment?"

"I spake thus to Gilebertus. How may we be certain it was her remedies that wrought his recovery? Was he not also blessed by the church's prayers? Perchance it was divine intervention that mended him, or mayhap he improved of his own accord."

"Believest thou that truly?"

"I knowest not what to believe now," Marcus replied with a heavy sigh.

"Wouldst thou fancy some tea, Marcus?" she inquired as she moved toward the pantry.

"Aye, something a bit more fortifying, my dear. Ah, never mind. I have it here already."

Cypress managed to push open a window. "Follow my lead," she said as she and Angel entered. They sat on the table facing Anabella. Cypress meowed softly, just loud enough for her to hear, her diamond-shaped patch of white fur clearly visible.

"Why, Cypress. What brings thee here?"

Cypress jumped to the floor. "We need to do something to tell her we need help." She paced around Anabella's feet. Angel jumped to the floor and followed suit.

Anabella knew and trusted Cypress completely. She knew that she and her strange-looking companion were trying to tell her something, but she was having a hard time knowing just what to do.

Cypress jumped back up on the table and looked her in the eyes with a pleading expression. Angel followed suit.

The connection between humans and their beloved animals became expansive, filling the room like Anabella had never felt before. She understood that there was great distress. She knew it had to be about Millie.

"By my troth, I will help thee. Lead me to what troubles you." Anabella said, then turned to Marcus. "Marcus, I have a minor errand. I must run."

He acknowledged her with a grunt.

Cypress, Angel, and Skittish led Anabella through the dimly lit streets of the township, arriving shortly at the livery. Anabella paused as the three cats stopped just outside the door.

Anabella was able to overhear Friar Rufus discussing plans to help Millie with several of the town's most upstanding citizens, the merchants of grain and textiles, those who knew and used the trade routes.

The meeting was highly secretive. Everyone was cautious because they feared the archbishop and they favored stability. But they were beginning to understand that some things were more important.

All those present owed their own or a loved one's health or even their very lives to Millie's healings. In the end, they had to ask themselves if they were brave enough to defy the authority of the church to help Millie escape.

"We must retain the utmost secrecy," said one of the attendees.

"Yes," said another. "The archbishop would be a powerful enemy. I do not wish to draw his ire."

"We must all bind ourselves to a covenant," declared another attendee. "None shall betray another. Swear unto me that thou shalt never reveal my name, come what may."

All consented and vowed silence.

After the last person had vowed silence, Anabella entered the livery. Everyone gasped. The mayor's wife had just overheard everything they had said!

Hearts raced, and heavy breathing could be heard throughout the room.

Raising her hand, Anabella said, "I, Anabella Marcus, hereby bind myself to this covenant. I swear that I shall never betray the name of any here, no matter what."

CHAPTER SEVEN:

HERETICS IN THE LIVERY

"Anabella, what brings thee hither?" said Friar Rufus.

"Tis the queerest tale, good friar, but truth be told, twas these cats that guided me here. Methinks, they sense the peril afoot for Millie. They beckoned with such earnestness, as if imploring me to follow them to this place."

Cypress, Angel, and Skittish sat calmly at Anabella's feet. Angel turned to Cypress. "I can see that they acknowledge us. We need to signal our intentions."

"I agree," said Skittish. "Knowing their true intent changes everything. I see that I have nothing to fear from them. Show us how to signal them, Cypress."

Cypress stood up. "Do as I do. This works with Millie, but it took a while for her to understand what I was doing. They may not know at first what we intend. You must be patient with them."

With that, Cypress walked over to the space between Anabella and Friar Rufus. She walked in small circles. Angel followed, making her own small circles next to Cypress. Skittish then joined in.

"Verily, I have naught beheld anything like this," Friar Rufus exclaimed. "Indeed, I recognize these cats. I espied them earlier this evening at Millie's cottage. You are all familiar with Cypress. Yet behold the unusual marks upon these other two. Never have I laid eyes upon such cats. Whence do they hail, and what message do they bear?"

"I cannot fathom," responded Anabella, "yet they display a keen wit, as if they are driven by a purpose and bear affection for Millie. Perchance the Almighty hath bestowed them upon us as a blessing."

"Or mayhap it is the work of the devil!" Patrick Foster, a grain merchant, declared from across the chamber, his gaze fixed intently on Cypress.

"I know his vibration," said Skittish. "It's like he is my human. I feel like I know him well, but I don't know just how."

"Follow your feelings, Skittish," said Cypress.

The room had fallen silent.

Skittish walked over to Patrick and sat in front of him. It all felt so familiar. He meowed and rubbed himself against Patrick's legs, back and forth. Patrick's expression softened. He picked Skittish up, and they looked each other in the eye.

"Verily, I feel a kinship with this cat," he declared. "Methinks I know him truly, though not since I was a boy have I kept a cat nor suffered one to dwell within my home. Our hounds would brook no such fellow. Yet, behold us now. What witchcraft plays upon us?" he said.

"Why wouldst thou deem such a lovely beast a servant of darkness, good sir?" Anabella questioned. "Behold him, for he offers naught but affection."

"And what of Cypress, the black 'devil' cat, as thou sayest? Art thou aware of her deeds for my kin?"

"Nay, I have not been told of such matters. What has this cat wrought?"

Anabella advanced to face him squarely, her voice firm yet laden with emotion. "Cypress, in concert with Millie, was the savior of my Robbie's life. When all seemed beyond hope and neither divine nor physician's aid availed, 'twas the sagacity of Millie and the counsel of Cypress that shepherded us from peril.

This cat is not an agent of malevolence but rather a luminary of hope."

Still holding Skittish, Patrick looked into the cat's eyes. Slowly, his grip softened, and he allowed Skittish to nuzzle closer. Skittish emitted a loud purr.

Anabella continued, "The tales spun about night creatures, omens, and witches—they are mere fables crafted to instill fear and exert control. Tonight, these cats have demonstrated their true place in our lives, a role rooted not in malevolence but in sincere affection."

Around the room, the tension dissipated as the townspeople watched the interaction between Patrick and Skittish.

Friar Rufus nodded slowly. "Perhaps we've judged too hastily, swayed by old wives' tales and sinister sermons. These creatures are more than mere pets. They are our allies, displaying a level of bravery and wit tonight by guiding Anabella here."

Patrick then added, setting Skittish down with care, "It seems we might be able to look beyond our fears and rally behind Millie."

Anabella smiled warmly at him then at those gathered. "This eve, we face a most crucial choice. We must secure Millie's safety. How shall we accomplish this?"

The meeting continued with a renewed sense of purpose and unity. Plans were laid to protect Millie from danger.

As the townspeople plotted their course of action, the three cats watched from the sidelines.

"They don't know how urgent it is to act now," Angel said. "They think they have more time. What do we do, Cypress?"

"I know a trick. Follow my lead." Cypress ran over to Anabella. Biting into her dress, she pulled her toward the door. Angel caught on. She trotted quickly over to Friar Rufus, latched onto a low-hanging part of his frock, and tugged. Skittish headed for Patrick, latched onto his pant leg, and pulled.

Anabella stepped into the center of the room, her voice clear and urgent. "Time is against us, and we cannot stand against the archbishop's influence. He holds sway over my husband, and I fear it won't be long before the constables come to arrest Millie. We need to move her out of the township swiftly."

Patrick responded, "I have access to my grain wagons. I can help transport her and her belongings. But where can we take her?"

"Verily, I am acquainted with a locale," Anabella replied. "Yon lies a brick cottage upon the forest's edge, just beyond Luton, a two-day travel to the north. It was once the dwelling of my dear departed parents, and now my sister Ruby and I do jointly hold its ownership. I shall pen a missive for thee to bear, ensuring all be made ready for Millie. Fear not, for it rests in seclusion, safe from prying eyes."

"Verily," declared Patrick, "a wagon shall await ere the morrow's dawn. I, myself, shall guide it forth, arriving at Millie's humble cottage with the sun's first rays. She must be prepared to depart at that early hour."

Friar Rufus nodded in agreement. "Indeed, it shall serve as her sanctuary."

The plan was set. They prepared for the swift and secret departure to whisk Millie away as soon as possible.

Friar Rufus and Anabella rushed back to Millie's cottage. A cluster of town constables stood guard outside the cottage, their stern faces betraying the deed already done.

"We are too late," Anabella murmured, her voice a mere breath against the stillness of the night. "They have already taken her."

Millie had indeed been taken into custody, her fate now in the hands of church guards who would not see beyond their blind obedience.

Anabella questioned one of the constables, one she was familiar with.

"Constable Luca, can you recount what transpired at Millie's house this eve?"

"Verily, Mayoress Anabella, a most grievous event hath unfolded. The church's sentinels have apprehended good Millie on charges most foul— witchery. Hath madness claimed their wits? Millie is a kind soul, ever aiding me with the afflictions of my rheum. I endeavored to stay their hands, yet they dismissed me, proclaiming 'twas the church's affair. Methinks she now languishes within the jail."

They all left immediately for the local jail. They arrived just as Mayor Marcus was leaving.

"Wait here, please, good friar," Anabella said to Rufus and walked over to Marcus. "Are you responsible for this travesty?"

"There is nothing I can do, my dearest. The archbishop wields the power of the holy church. I would be a fool to oppose him on this."

From their hiding place, Cypress's ears flattened against her head. "Millie is inside that building."

Skittish's tail twitched with agitation, and Angel's gaze turned steely in the dim light.

CHAPTER EIGHT:

CAPTURED

In the cold embrace of the local jail, a single dim lantern cast elongated shadows on the walls where Millie sat, huddled in a corner of her cell. Her hands clasped tightly together, fingers intertwined with the beads of her rosary, as silent tears traced the contours of a face etched with despair. The familiar comfort of her cottage seemed a world away, replaced by the harsh reality of stone and iron.

As the heavy door creaked open, Millie was escorted to a bare room. A table and two chairs were its only furnishings, an austere setting for the grim proceedings to come. She was seated, her hands resting on the cold, rough surface of the table.

Across from her, the church's guards—faces grim and compassionless.

The interrogation began, not with questions but with a search for the supposed devil's mark, a sign that would "confirm" her guilt in the eyes of her accusers. Her protests fell on deaf ears as the guards carried out their orders.

As the long hours of the night stretched endlessly, Millie was deprived of sleep by the relentless questioning and accusations of the church's interrogators. These men, skilled in the cruel arts of extracting confessions, sought to break her spirit and turn her own words against her in a twisted semblance of justice. The town constables, familiar with Millie's compassion and wisdom, stood aside, their presence merely a façade to give the appearance of conforming to civil laws. The church's guardsmen, who had no qualms about carrying out their brutal duty, had usurped them, determined to fulfill their grim task.

In the small hours, when the night was at its darkest, Millie's resolve waned. Exhaustion clouded her thoughts, and the relentless pursuit of a confession weighed heavily on her soul. Yet, the flame of hope flickered stubbornly within her, refusing to be extinguished.

Standing vigil outside the jail, Anabella, Friar Rufus, and the three cats regrouped with the others, their minds racing against time to formulate a new plan of rescue. Each understood the consequences if they failed to act.

Lurking in the darkness just beyond the jail, they remained unnoticed as they watched Mayor Marcus emerge from the building. His usual composed demeanor was replaced by a noticeable tremor of horror and dismay.

The brutal interrogation had yielded what they considered damning evidence. They had established "stigma Diabolicum," the devil's mark, beyond all doubt. Millie was found to have multiple moles and skin tags, each examined with morbid fascination. To the interrogators, these blemishes were not mere marks of nature but signs of her unholy pact. Even more damning was the discovery of a patch of insensitive skin that would not bleed—a trait believed to be from Satan himself as a mark of their covenant. This insensitivity to pain was taken as undeniable proof of her allegiance to the devil and her practice of witchcraft, sealing her fate in the eyes of her accusers.

Anabella stepped forward from the veil of night, her voice barely a whisper yet sharp as a blade. "Marcus, what have you allowed? Can you even grasp the magnitude of this?"

He looked at her, his voice faltering as he replied, "Joy is far from my heart, my dear. The weight of this night's actions lies sore upon me. My pleas for her gentle handling were cast aside. It seems I wield no sway to shield her. At least, the interrogation is over. The church's guards are satisfied with their evidence and have left."

Their eyes locked, a silent conversation of shared disappointment. Anabella's gaze was filled with a mix of accusation and sorrow.

L.S. Tucker

CHAPTER NINE:

THE ESCAPE

Archbishop Gilebertus entered Millie's cell, his imposing figure casting a long, intimidating shadow against the flickering torchlight. He moved with deliberate slowness, each step echoing ominously off the stone walls.

Millie sat on her stone bench, tightly clutching her rosary beads. As the archbishop approached, she looked up, her eyes weary but resolute. Despite the hours of torment, her spirit remained unbroken.

"Millie," Gilebertus began, his voice cold and steely, "you stand accused of heresy and blasphemy for daring to challenge the authority of the Holy Church."

Millie met his gaze, her expression unwavering. "I have committed no wrongdoing, Your Grace," she replied firmly yet respectfully. "I have only endeavored to heal and aid those in need."

"Your defiance is noted," Gilebertus said, his tone sharpening. "But it is not for you to question the Church. Confess your sins, admit your consort with the Devil, and perhaps you may yet find mercy.

"I consort with no devil," Millie replied, her grip on the rosary tightening. "My hands have toiled solely to heal, never to harm. The Lord stands as my witness."

Gilebertus's eyes narrowed, his patience thinning. "Your silence and stubbornness will not save you. Confess now or face divine retribution."

Millie took a deep breath, her resolve hardening. "I have nothing to confess," she spoke quietly, though with a hint of defiance. "I place my trust in God's mercy, not in the cruelty of men."

Gilebertus stepped closer, his face inches from hers, his eyes blazing with righteous fury. "Your arrogance will be your undoing," he hissed. "The Church is the arbiter of God's will on earth, and you shall not escape its judgment."

Millie closed her eyes, her lips moving silently in prayer. "Lord, give me strength," she whispered, her voice barely audible, as she held her rosary beads to her lips.

"How dare you, a witch, a consort of the devil, lay your unholy hands upon those sacred beads?" Archbishop Gilebertus thundered, his voice reverberating through the stone cell.

With a swift and brutal motion, he snatched the rosary from Millie's hands, breaking the strands, sending the beads scattering across the cold, unforgiving floor. Each bead echoed her anguish as it bounced and rolled away, lost in the dim corners of her cell.

Millie cried in despair, her sobs mingling with whispered prayers. "O Lord, bestow upon me Thy strength," she pleaded, tears streaming down her face. Her fingers, empty and trembling, clutched at the air where her rosary had been, seeking solace in the emptiness left behind.

"God will offer no salvation to a witch, Millie," Gilebertus sneered.

Despite the overwhelming despair, Millie felt a flicker of hope within her heart. She closed her eyes and took a deep breath, her sorrow transforming into anger, and anger turned into determination. Hope turned to belief, and belief to knowing. Centering herself amidst the chaos, she realized that the true strength of her faith lay not in the beads but in her unwavering devotion.

With renewed resolve, Millie turned her body and straightened her back to meet her tormentor's gaze, her eyes burning with defiance. "You may break my body, but you will never break my spirit," she declared, her voice steady and strong. "My faith in God is unyielding, and His mercy is boundless."

The archbishop's smirk faltered, his confident facade cracking for a moment. For the first time, the power dynamics shifted, and it was Millie who stood stronger. Her words, filled with conviction, illuminating the darkness that sought to consume her, casting a radiant light that seemed to push back against the archbishop's oppressive presence.

Gilebertus, taken aback by her unbroken spirit, took a step back. He had expected her to crumble, to yield to his authority, but instead, she stood resolute, her faith shining brightly. The sight unsettled him, planting a seed of doubt in his mind.

Millie's eyes never left the archbishop's face, her defiance unwavering. "You may hold power over my physical form, but my soul belongs to God, and His judgment is the only one I fear."

Unknown to Gilebertus, his cherished cat, Purity, sat watching from the deep shadows, a silent witness to the night's grim events. With a graceful leap, Purity entered the cell, the soft thud of his landing a stark contrast to the harsh words being spoken. He moved with purpose, settling himself on Millie's lap, his gaze locking with the archbishop's.

Gilebertus reached to retrieve his pet but was met with a hiss and a sharp bite to his finger, a crimson bead of blood emerging as testimony to the betrayal. The archbishop stood frozen.

The cell fell silent, the only sound was the soft drip of blood falling to the stone floor. Gilebertus's eyes, wide with shock, met those of his cat once more. Purity hissed again, a clear renunciation of allegiance, before turning and vanishing into the night.

Finally, with a heavy sigh that spoke volumes of the confusion and introspection that consumed him, Archbishop Gilebertus departed. The echoes of his retreating footsteps were a somber melody to the ponderous thoughts that plagued his mind.

Constable Luca excused himself from the tension-filled cell. As he stepped out into the embrace of the night, he took in deep breaths of the cooler air. He noticed Mayor Marcus and Anabella engaged in hushed conversation nearby. "Good evening, my lord." he said, tipping his hat respectfully. "I didst witness a most strange occurrence. The archbishop's very own cat, always so docile and affectionate, turned upon him—bit him and drew blood there within the very confines of the cell."

Anabella and Marcus exchanged glances of disbelief. "Be that so?" Anabella murmured.

Her gaze drifted downward to the three feline figures at her feet. "What an extraordinary thing," she mused aloud. "It doth make one ponder if these small creatures are not more than just mere animals."

The constable looked down at the cats, his expression softening. "If even the creatures do rise against the archbishop, perchance there's more at play than doth meet the eye."

Anabella kneeled, her hand gently brushing over Cypress's fur. "Perchance there be more surprises yet to unfold," she whispered.

Cypress let out a soft meow, and the other two cats closed in, forming a small circle around Anabella's feet—a silent pact of solidarity.

After Constable Luca returned to his post in the jail, Friar Rufus approached Mayor Marcus and Anabella. "Begging your pardon, Your lord. Wouldst it be possible for me to speak to the prisoner?"

Rufus did not have any real plan. It was an impulsive act. He only knew he needed to do something, anything.

"I canst think of no cause to deny thee, good friar. Of course, thou mayst speak with her. I shall escort thee."

The mayor led the way through the dim corridors of the jailhouse, his footsteps echoing in the oppressive silence.

In the commotion of the moment, Cypress, Angel, and Skittish slipped in unnoticed just as the door swung shut, their agile bodies finding cover among the shadows and corners as they followed the two men to Millie. They watched attentively as Rufus was granted entry to Millie's cell.

"Your Honor, might I request some privacy for mine counsel with the prisoner?"

Mayor Marcus nodded. "Of course, Friar Rufus. I shall step out."

He left Rufus and Millie alone in the cell, her gentle sobs breaking the silence.

Angel of the Dark Ages

Rufus kneeled beside Millie, taking her hands in his. "Millie, we must be brave," he whispered. "A trial by water awaits at noon, and we cannot let it come to pass."

In the shadows of a dark corridor, Cypress cast a glance toward Angel and Skittish, concern furrowing her brow.

"My dark fur would draw too much concern from the guards," she murmured. "Do either of you have an idea?"

Angel cleared her mind. If ever her guidance was needed, now was the time. Her eyes gleamed with sudden inspiration. "I might," she replied.

Angel shifted her gaze to the constable guarding the cell, noting the ambivalence in his aura. She edged closer to him and stepped out of the shadows.

Her striking Siamese markings drew the constable's gaze in sheer amazement as they glowed even in the dim light of the jail.

"What manner of beast be this? Never hath I observed such fur," he exclaimed, his focus shifting from duty to curiosity. "Hector. Looketh at this strange cat."

The guard was very intrigued with her appearance and attempted to draw her closer. Angel jumped onto the tabletop, always staying just out of reach and daring the guard to grab her. He took the bait, and she drew him farther and farther from his post.

77

Skittish followed suit, stepping into the light and presenting himself in full view so that Hector could see, daring him to catch him but always remaining just out of reach. Both guards were now fully engaged in the activity. They knocked over buckets and mugs, talking loudly to one another as they attempted to capture the elusive cats.

"Now, Millie, we flee," Rufus whispered.

With Millie's arm around his shoulder, Rufus hurried her toward the exit, moving through the dimly lit corridors of the jail, passing the distracted guards.

Finally, at the end of the last corridor, they encountered a locked door. Millie sobbed.

"Have faith, Millie," said the friar.

Stepping out from around the corner, Constable Luca stared at Millie intently and swallowed hard. He stood there for what seemed like forever. Finally, pulling the keys from his belt, he unlocked the door and stepped inside the corridor, walking past Millie and Friar Rufus as if he had not seen them.

The constable muttered to himself, "Whence cometh such uproar yonder? I am bound to seeketh its source." Then, he proceeded toward the back of the jail, leaving the door open and unattended.

Followed silently by the three cats, Millie and Rufus slipped through the door and finally to freedom outside.

The stern voice of Archbishop Gilebertus immediately shattered the night air.

"Whither dost thou wander, good friar? And who be this person in your company?"

Beside him stood two formidable church soldiers, their faces as hard as the stone walls.

Friar Rufus felt a chill run down his spine as the soldiers stepped forward, seizing him and Millie with cruel harshness. The cold metal shackles applied tightly around their wrists, a stark symbol of their sudden and harsh captivity. Millie's heart raced, her breath quickening as she strained against the chains, the reality of their predicament sinking in.

"Unbind her!" Rufus demanded, his voice shaking with a mix of anger and desperation. "She has committed no wrong!"

The archbishop's eyes narrowed, a vindictive smile playing on his lips. "You are ill-placed to issue commands, good friar. This woman standeth accused of sorcery, and thou art now accused of aiding her. Both of ye shall answer for thy transgressions."

Millie's eyes filled with fear, yet she held her head high, refusing to show weakness before her accuser. "I am no witch," she declared, her voice steady despite her trembling hands. "I have only ever sought to mend and aid those in need."

Gilebertus laughed, a harsh, mocking sound. "Thy words hold little sway now, sorceress. The holy church shall determine thy fate."

The soldiers marched them through the darkened streets, their destination the dungeons of the abbey, the weight of the shackles a constant reminder of their perilous situation. Millie felt a flicker of hope as she saw a shadow move in the corner of her vision—Cypress, Angel, and Skittish were following them, their eyes gleaming with determination. They were not alone in this fight, and that knowledge gave her the strength to keep going.

Archbishop Gilebertus gazed with a mix of pity and scorn at Friar Rufus, shackled in the dim cell adjacent to Millie's.

"You have cast your lot with the devil's schemes, Rufus," the archbishop proclaimed gravely. "What has led ye to defy the church? Has this supposed healer ensnared thou with her sorcery?"

"Thou knowest full well, as do I, that Millie harboreth no maleficence," retorted Friar Rufus, his voice steady. "Her life's work is nothing but kindness and succor. Wouldst thou condemn her to the gallows for such noble deeds? If so, taketh my life as well, and let us then discern who truly basks in the devil's gloom."

Gilebertus screamed, "Thou blasphemous heretic! Thy boldness to address me thus shall be your undoing. Thou shalt share this witch's fiery fate!"

CHAPTER TEN:

THE TRIAL

High in the rafters of the abbey's great hall, four cats watched the proceedings unfold. Hidden from sight, Purity looked away in sadness.

"Are we helpless before these events?" Cypress asked, her voice heavy with despair. "Is there anything that can be done?"

Determination blazing in her eyes, Angel seated herself directly in front of Cypress. "Look at me, my soulmate. If indeed I am gifted with foresight and intuition, then we both are. It is time we called upon this gift together. Look at me. Look at me, and do not falter. Ask for guidance."

A long moment passed as they held each other's gaze. Cypress's eyes, filled with a mixture of hope and knowing, met Angel's unwavering stare. Their connection deepened as they focused their thoughts, and the air between them became charged with a silent communication that only they could understand.

Purity and Skittish joined them. The area they encircled glowed softly, a radiant aura that seemed to pulse with their combined energy. They all smiled, a shared understanding blossoming between them. A thought occurred to them all, and without a word, they knew it. It was as if a veil had lifted, revealing a path forward that had been hidden in plain sight.

As the light faded, they all knew what to do. Cypress turned to Purity and said, "Come with me." Together, they ran across the ceiling beams, taking their positions.

Angel looked at Skittish. "Let's go," she said.

They all knew the plan and their parts in it. The time for action had come. They moved with purpose, their minds clear and focused. For Millie, for Friar Rufus, and for the justice that had to prevail.

The grand hall of the abbey was filled to the brim with townsfolk, clergy, and members of the council, their faces a mix of curiosity and apprehension. The air was thick with tension as everyone awaited the trial. Millie, with chains around her wrists, stood in the center, flanked by two stern-looking church soldiers. Friar Rufus, also shackled, stood beside her, his expression one of grim determination.

Archbishop Gilebertus, dressed in his most imposing ecclesiastical robes, approached the pulpit. His face was a mask of righteous indignation, and his eyes blazed with fervor. The room fell silent as he raised his hands, commanding attention.

"Beloved brethren in Christ. We are gathered here to purge the evil that has taken hold in our midst," he began, his voice booming through the hall. "These two souls, Millie and Friar Rufus, stand accused of witchcraft and heresy—vile practices that corrupt the soul and imperil our very way of life."

He paused, allowing his words to settle upon the assembly before continuing with greater fervor. "For years, Millie has masqueraded as a healer, beguiling you with her charms and potions. And Friar Rufus, who should have been a shepherd to his flock, has instead chosen to consort with this witch, aiding and abetting her in her dark deeds. But I say unto you, these remedies and teachings are but the tools of the devil! We have found upon Millie's body the marks of Satan himself, proof of her unholy pact, and Friar Rufus has been complicit in spreading her malevolence."

Millie stood firm; her eyes unyielding despite the weight of his accusations. Friar Rufus, though weary, remained resolute. The council members shifted uneasily, their discomfort growing with each vehement statement from the archbishop.

"As your spiritual leader, it is my sacred duty to purge this community of their wickedness," Gilebertus continued, his voice rising to a fever pitch. "We must not be swayed by their false piety or the seeming benevolence of their actions. Evil often wears a pleasing guise to beguile the innocent."

"This woman," he continued, pointing an accusatory finger at Millie, "stands accused of witchcraft, heresy, and consorting with the devil. She has used her unholy powers to deceive and corrupt the innocent, to turn them away from the light of our Lord."

The townsfolk shifted uncomfortably, murmuring among themselves. Millie's friends and supporters looked stricken, while those few who had always viewed her with suspicion nodded grimly.

Just as the archbishop was about to launch into the crescendo of his diatribe, a black shadow darted across the floor. Cypress, sleek and black, appeared at the archbishop's feet. A ripple of whispers and gasps spread through the assembly.

With deliberate grace, Cypress rubbed herself affectionately against Gilebertus's leg. The archbishop's face turned crimson with rage.

"Away with you, fiend!" he bellowed, attempting to kick the cat. Cypress nimbly dodged the blow, her movements fluid and effortless.

The crowd watched in stunned silence as the archbishop's attempts to rid himself of the cat grew increasingly frantic. Each time he lunged, Cypress evaded him with ease, darting just out of reach and then returning to rub herself against his leg affectionately and meow loudly. The scene was comical and humiliating, casting a shadow of doubt over the archbishop's authority.

"This is the devil's work!" Gilebertus shouted, his voice cracking. "A trick to undermine the righteous path we tread. Do not be deceived by this creature!"

Friar Rufus could not contain his amusement. A hearty laugh burst from his lips, breaking the tension in the room. "Cypress, you rascal," he chuckled, shaking his head. His laughter proved contagious, and soon, many in the assembly were laughing as well.

The archbishop's face turned an even deeper shade of red as he struggled to regain control of the situation. "Silence!" he roared, his voice barely audible over the laughter. "This be no laughing matter!"

Cypress finally retreated, but it took several minutes for the laughter to subside, leaving the archbishop visibly shaken and humiliated. Cypress sat nearby on a rafter well out of reach, mewing loudly every time the archbishop began to speak, causing sporadic laughter among the crowd.

Suddenly, a stir of movement caught the eyes of the assembly. Purity, the archbishop's own beloved white cat, appeared in the rafters beside Cypress.

Gilebertus, desperately trying to maintain his composure, continued his fervent diatribe. "Silence!" he roared, but his voice was barely audible over the escalating laughter. "This be no laughing matter!" he repeated. The hall echoed with sounds of amusement.

As the archbishop tried to regain control, Cypress began to moan in a low, continuous tone, an eerie sound that immediately drew attention. Purity joined in, his voice harmonizing with Cypress's. Their combined moaning built, rising and falling in a haunting, angelic harmony that seemed to vibrate the very walls of the great hall. The acoustics amplified this ethereal chorus, making the entire building resonate deeply within the hearts of everyone present.

Angel and Skittish added their voices to the strange melody, creating a sound that was otherworldly, like the music of angels descending from the heavens. The celestial tones filled the great hall with a sense of awe and wonder, casting a spell over the assembly. It was as if the air itself had become charged with divine presence.

Silence fell over the assembly as the celestial tones came to a sudden and synchronistic stop. All four cats, clearly visible, stared silently at the crowd. The hall stood in stunned quietude.

Gilebertus, his face contorted with rage and mortification, struggled to regain his authority. He pointed a trembling finger at the cats, his voice cracking as he shouted, "This be a trick, a sorcery to deceive you all!"

But his words rang hollow in the profound silence.

The archbishop's attempts to blame the devil now seemed desperate and unconvincing. The people exchanged glances, their expressions a mix of disbelief and curiosity.

The archbishop turned and glared at the council, his eyes blazing with barely contained fury. "The evidence is irrefutable. Stigma Diabolicum! She bears the marks of the devil upon her body—moles and patches of insensitive skin, untouched by the pain that afflicts true believers. These are the signs of her covenant with darkness. You must find them guilty! For the sake of our faith and our community, we cannot allow this evil to persist."

The council hesitated but ultimately nodded in agreement. None dared to oppose him outright.

As Millie and Friar Rufus were led away, their fate seemingly sealed by the archbishop's command, a seed of doubt had been firmly planted in the hearts of all in the assembly, and the damage was considerable. In the minds of those present, suspicion seethed.

Gilebertus won his verdict, but someone else won the case.

CHAPTER ELEVEN:

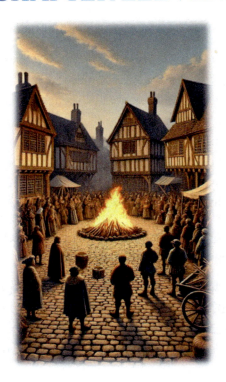

THE EXECUTION

A proclamation echoed through the township, announcing the impending execution. All residents were summoned to bear witness, the event presented almost as a macabre form of public entertainment.

In the town square, preparations for the execution were underway. A bonfire was being meticulously prepared, its flames destined to climb to the evening sky. At the center, two stakes had been erected, signaling the ominous fate awaiting Millie and Friar Rufus. As the townspeople assembled, an air of somber anticipation hung over the crowd.

Cypress, Angel, Skittish, and Purity mingled silently with the onlookers. Their presence went largely unnoticed as the townsfolk's attention was drawn to the unfolding spectacle. As dusk settled, a cart creaked forward from the church's back gate. Inside, Millie and Friar Rufus sat bound and caged, their faces etched with resignation. The cart slowly made its way toward the town square.

Ordinarily, such a procession would be met with jeers and mockery—a cruel tradition from over a century of witch trials that had desensitized the populace to such horrors. But this evening was different. There were no laughs, no taunts. Instead, a profound silence enveloped the crowd, sensing the gravity of the injustice.

Whispers rippled through the assembly as the cart approached the bonfire. Groups of townspeople exchanged hushed conversations, their faces reflecting confusion and doubt.

"Did you see what transpired at the trial?" one man murmured to his neighbor.

"Aye, the cats—they sang like angels," replied the neighbor, his voice tinged with awe. "'Twas as if the heavens themselves had intervened."

"Could it be a sign?" another woman wondered aloud. "Perhaps they are not witches after all. How could the devil produce such a divine sound? And right there within the Lord's own house."

"Indeed," an elderly man nodded thoughtfully. "I have witnessed many trials, yet never have I seen the like. Those cats…they stirred something within me. It was as if they were speaking directly to my soul."

The cart halted abruptly next to the prepared woodpile. Archbishop Gilebertus, having just arrived in his ornate carriage, stepped out to observe the grim proceedings. Two church guards roughly dragged Friar Rufus from the cart, holding him upright while he bowed his head in defeat. Millie, too, was yanked from her seat, treated just as brutally.

"Look at them," a young woman whispered to her friend. "They appear not as witches, but as we do, like our own neighbors."

"They've helped so many of us," her friend replied, her voice breaking. "Millie saved my sister's life with her herbs. And Friar Rufus…he's been a pillar of our community."

Unable to bear the sight any longer, Cypress released a piercing screech and leaped at the guard manhandling her mistress. Angel followed suit, launching herself at the other guard with a fierce cry, her claws finding purchase on his exposed arms. Skittish and Purity, showing no hesitation, leaped upon the guards holding Friar Rufus, their sharp teeth sinking deeply into any exposed flesh.

Their actions sent a palpable shock through the crowd. Suddenly, a woman's scream cut through the air, "Let them go!"

Her cry, filled with desperation and fury, ignited the crowd. One by one, voices joined in, the chant swelling into a roaring demand. Driven by a newfound resolve, the crowd surged forward, overwhelming the guards.

In the chaos, quick-thinking townspeople dashed to Rufus's side, one of them slicing through his bonds as another rescuer did the same for Millie. Pandemonium swept through the square as the townspeople, emboldened by the bravery of the cats and their shared sense of justice, turned against the authorities.

"We cannot let this happen!" shouted a man from the front of the crowd, his fists clenched in defiance. "They be innocent!"

"Down with the false accusers!" another yelled, rallying the crowd. "We stand with Millie and Friar Rufus!" Amidst the turmoil, Cypress, Angel, Skittish, and Purity watched with a sense of triumph. They had not only saved their human companions but had also awakened the true spirit of the community. The celestial tones they had produced had done more than disrupt the trial; they had planted seeds of doubt and hope that were now blossoming into a powerful call for justice.

As Millie and Friar Rufus were led to safety by the townspeople, the bonfire remained unlit, its flames never to consume the innocent. The air, once heavy with anticipation of death, was now filled with the collective breath of a community awakened to its own power and humanity.

Amidst the uproar, Purity calmly emerged from the crowd and approached Archbishop Gilebertus, seating himself squarely in front of him. He fixed him with a steady, piercing gaze. Gilebertus looked down at his inflamed finger, then back at Purity, tears beginning to streak down his cheeks. Then, Purity stood, and with a dignified turn, he walked away from the archbishop, melding back into the crowd that was erupting in a defiant fight for justice.

Overwhelmed by the sea of familiar faces—mothers, fathers, siblings, cousins, and friends—the church's guards found themselves incapable of raising their weapons against them.

As the guards were subdued, the chaos provided the perfect cover for Millie and Friar Rufus to escape. Guided by a few brave souls, they slipped into the labyrinthine alleyways that snaked through the darker parts of the township.

The archbishop remained frozen in place, his eyes wide and his mouth agape as the town square erupted into chaos around him. The betrayal of his own beloved cat, Purity, had cut deeper than any rebuke or defiance from his flock. He watched, powerless, as the crowd spirited Millie and Friar Rufus away from their impending doom.

Millie and Rufus, escorted by a small group of brave citizens, moved quickly, disappearing into a narrow alley to the north of the square, blending into the shadows of the evening.

Across the tumultuous crowd, the captain of the guard called out to the archbishop, his voice cutting through the noise. "Did you see where they went?"

The archbishop paused for a long, heavy moment. His gaze drifted across the chaotic scene. Finally, he raised a hand, pointing deliberately in the opposite direction of Millie and Rufus's escape. "They fled that way," he lied, indicating a street south of the square.

The captain rallied his guards and led them away in haste toward the south.

As the guards' footsteps faded, and the departing crowd erupted in cheers, Archbishop Gilebertus stood alone in the empty square—alone except for an old pure white cat, who sat facing him.

CHAPTER TWELVE:

A NEW BEGINNING

Concealed by the shadows to the north of town, Millie and Rufus met up with Patrick, the grain trader, who had been waiting, ready to lend his aid. Breathless from his hurried approach, he gestured toward a nearby cart piled high with sacks of grain.

"Quickly!" he urged, his voice low and urgent. "Hide beneath the covers. We're leaving right now."

Without hesitation, the small group swiftly hid Millie and Rufus beneath the heavy burlap sacks, ensuring that no prying eyes could see them. Patrick climbed aboard, casting one last look over his shoulder to ensure no one had noticed their stealthy escape. As the cart rolled quietly into the night, heading toward the safety of the countryside, three cats silently boarded the cart and hid themselves among the sacks of grain.

Everything had been meticulously planned. Anabella had written a detailed letter to her sister Ruby Gill in Luton. It laid out the entire situation, explaining the dire circumstances Millie and Friar Rufus found themselves in. She requested sanctuary for them in the secluded cottage on the edge of the forest that they jointly owned.

The trek was arduous, spanning nearly two days, yet remarkably, they encountered no guards or constables along the way. Their escape unfolded with an ease that belied the danger of their situation.

Once they had traversed the open countryside and put a significant distance between themselves and the township, Millie and Rufus emerged from hiding. The fresh air and the safety of distance helped Millie recover her composure. Eventually, they paused to enjoy a modest breakfast, their first relaxed meal since the ordeal began.

Patrick Foster, who had taken it upon himself to ensure their safe passage, was at the reins of the wagon. His steady hands guided them along less-traveled paths, further ensuring their safety from any pursuers. As they ate, the small group shared a moment of gratitude for their current peace yet remained vigilant of the journey still ahead.

As they settled for breakfast, Cypress, Angel, and Skittish finally felt safe enough to come out from their hiding places within the wagon. With a graceful leap, they landed softly on the ground. Millie's face lit up with joy. She couldn't contain the delighted scream that burst forth. Cypress dashed into her open arms, and they shared a heartfelt embrace, a reunion filled with warmth and relief.

While Angel observed the touching scene, Skittish's curiosity drew him toward Patrick. With tentative steps, he approached and gently rubbed himself against Patrick's legs. Patrick, taken aback, hesitated at first. As a boy, he had once owned a cat. But now, his experiences were limited to the feral cats that roamed his farm, keeping the rodent and pest populations under control. His home was a place for dogs, and the cats were usually distant observers rather than affectionate companions.

Looking down at Skittish, who seemed to have just claimed him as his own, Patrick couldn't help but smile, a bit bemused by the situation. "Well...it would seem I have a cat now," he remarked with a chuckle. This simple act of acceptance seemed to seal a new bond—one that promised a new friendship he hadn't anticipated.

Friar Rufus watched the unfolding scene with a smile. "He certainly seems taken with you, Patrick. How dost thou think thy wife will react?"

Patrick scratched his head, still watching Skittish with a mix of amusement and uncertainty. "I'm not entirely sure. I know not if he hath chosen to stay with me permanently. But if he doth choose, he shall be welcome at my abode. Verily, the hounds must need to grow accustomed to him."

"Verily, in days of yore, when I was but a young squire, I kept a feline companion. I cherished him dearly, and my heart was heavy with sorrow upon his passing."

"As thou hast recounted, this one is a stout-hearted scrapper. He didst confront two of the church guards and acquitted himself most admirably."

"Verily, it be true, the wretched souls suffereth greatly." Friar Rufus laughed.

Patrick chuckled softly, a new respect in his eyes as he regarded Skittish, who seemed content to linger by his side. The straightforward exchange indicated a potential change in his household's dynamics, but Patrick appeared receptive to it because of the little cat's bravery and loyalty.

With little time to spare, the group quickly finished their breakfast and resumed their journey. Now that they felt safer, everyone enjoyed the fresh air and the warm sunlight as they traveled through the picturesque countryside. Skittish chose to sit with Patrick, staking claim to a spot by his side.

Angel watched this developing bond with keen interest. "So, what's the story between you and your new human brother?" she inquired gently.

Skittish glanced at Patrick with a look of deep familiarity and then back at Angel. "I recognize him. I feel we have a long history. In past lives, I feel like he was often a woman or a child, but this time a man, always kind and nurturing. I didn't realize until now how much I've missed being around this human soul."

"Is that why April's mother needed to become allergic to you? To ensure this would not happen?"

"Yes, you are right," Skittish replied sheepishly.

"So, won't this delay your journey to become a greater cat?"

"Yes, it will. But so what if it does? We have all of eternity to play with, don't we?"

Angel sensed the rightness of the unexpected reunion.

On the second day, as dusk began to settle, their journey ended in a small but growing village of Luton, where Anabella's sister, Ruby Gill, resided. Her home was a large brick residence along the main street.

Having passed this way many times delivering his grain, this home was already familiar to Patrick. It was the home of Noah Gill, the wealthy owner of Gill's Brickyard. After a respectful knock, he awaited an answer.

A tall male servant responded from within. "Who shall I say is calling, sir?"

"Forgive my intrusion. I am Patrick Foster, a grain merchant. I seek Ruby Gill. I bear a missive from her sister, Anabella."

"Very well. Please wait here, sir. I shall call the mistress."

In a moment, Ruby, both startled and expectant, looked out. "Oh, heavens! Are all matters in order?" she exclaimed, her countenance reflecting deep worry.

"All is well with your sister and her kin, madam," Patrick assured her, offering the letter. "Yet, it is imperative that you peruse this missive forthwith."

"Oh my! Please, come in, Mr. Foster."

With trembling hands, Ruby tore open the envelope. Anabella had prepared the letter explaining the situation, ready for the moment Millie and Friar Rufus might escape.

"Oh my," Ruby murmured repeatedly as her eyes scanned the contents, the weight of the news sinking in.

After a few intense moments, she lifted her gaze from the letter, a resolve firming in her eyes.

"Millie and Friar Rufus may avail themselves of Mother's cottage for as long as necessary. Pray, enter, and take your ease," she insisted warmly, stepping aside to usher them in.

Ruby swung wide the large oak door and gestured invitingly to those still aboard the wagon.

"Please, come in. You are all welcome here," Ruby said, her voice warm and inviting.

Turning to her husband, who had joined her at the doorway, she continued, "Noah, do you remember the skilled healer Anabella always spoke of? This is her—Millie. She's the one who saved little Robbie."

Noah's face lit up with recognition and gratitude. "Verily, fair Millie, we have heard much of thee. We give thee thanks for rescuing our nephew," he exclaimed, extending a warm hand toward her. The firm grip of his handshake was accompanied by a sincere smile that spoke of his deep appreciation.

As they stepped inside, the guests could feel the warmth of the house embracing them, a stark contrast to the cool night outside. The rich scent of burning wood from a large hearth in the adjacent room mixed with the aroma of fresh herbs and baked goods, creating an atmosphere of comfort and abundance.

The room was adorned with tapestries depicting scenes of the countryside, and plush rugs covered the floors, muffling their footsteps. A large, inviting sofa with velvet cushions sat near the hearth, offering a place of rest and comfort. The flickering flames of the fire cast a cozy glow, and the soft crackle of burning logs added to the homey ambiance.

Noah turned and instructed a maid, who appeared from a side door, her apron dusted with flour from recent baking. "Louisa, pray see that our guests are provided with food and refreshment."

"Aye, Master Noah," Louisa replied.

"Will meat pie and mulberry juice be to your liking, good sir?" she asked Patrick, her voice carrying the practiced grace of a well-trained servant.

"The meat pie shall be most delightful, and the mulberry juice will suffice for Mistress Millie and Friar Rufus. Yet, I wonder, might there be some mead for my drink?"

"Indeed, good sir. I shall bring it forth anon." Louisa replied before curtsying and hurrying off to the kitchen.

As they ushered Millie and Friar Rufus inside, Ruby revealed the contents of the letter from her sister Anabella to Noah.

"Millie and this good friar have narrowly escaped the cruel witch hunts orchestrated by the church," she explained. "Anabella has requested they use Mother's cottage as a refuge."

She smiled reassuringly at her guests. "Verily, I did inform them that they might tarry as long as their need requireth."

"Verily, my dear, as I have spoken afore, thy mother's cottage belongeth to thee and Anabella. It is thine to wield as thou dost desire."

After their meal, they all settled into the plush seats near the fire. The guests could feel the stress of their journey melting away. The house filled with a sense of relief as the soothing warmth of the fire, and the soft hum of conversation continued well into the night. Three cats made themselves at home in the company of their humans.

CHAPTER THIRTEEN:

MILLIE'S NEW HOME

After a good night's sleep and a hearty breakfast, the small caravan made its way to the secluded cottage nestled near the edge of the woods. Patrick's sturdy grain wagon carried Millie, Friar Rufus, and the cats, while Ruby led the way on her horse, setting a gentle pace through the quiet morning. The air was filled with the fresh scent of pine and earth—a peaceful welcome.

Patrick carefully assisted Millie down from the wagon, offering a supportive arm as she stepped onto the soft forest floor. Rufus followed, his boots landing with a soft thud, and Cypress and Angel gracefully leaped down to explore their new surroundings.

"There's another one of those strange cats, isn't there?" Patrick remarked, looking back at the wagon. Skittish, however, remained perched on the edge, observing everything calmly.

"Come on now," Patrick coaxed, but Skittish made no move to join the others. Instead, Angel, concerned for her brother, hopped back onto the wagon.

"Are you not coming with us, Brother?" she asked, her voice tinged with worry.

"No, I am not. I belong with the man Patrick. We've shared many wonderful lives together, and I want my last life as a domestic cat to be with him. The Great Cat has promised that when I complete this mission, I will become a big and powerful wildcat in a place called Africa. Millie is safe. Our mission is accomplished. The Great Cat also said that we should enjoy each of our lives to the fullest and not waste any of them. I have a good number of years left. And so, I wish to spend them with Patrick."

Angel nuzzled her brother goodbye, her eyes soft with affection. "I will miss you. Perhaps I will see you again."

"I hope so, Sister. Goodbye."

With those final words, Angel leaped back to the ground, joining the others as they watched Skittish sit beside Patrick, who scratched the cat behind the ears with a smile as the wagon continued its journey to market.

As they crossed the threshold into the cottage, Ruby welcomed Millie with open arms, her voice warm with the promise of sanctuary. The air inside was stale, carrying the silence of months of being unoccupied, but it was soon filled with the sounds of life as they set about making the cottage habitable.

Together, Millie, Friar Rufus, and Ruby dusted off the old furniture, swept the floors, and lit a fire, each motion restoring warmth to the cold space.

Ruby showed Millie and Rufus around the quaint cottage.

"This here be the kitchen," she explained, opening drawers and cabinets to reveal their contents. "And the hearth doth keep the chill at bay during the cold nights."

The cottage, once belonging to Ruby's parents, Jakub and Hope Jones, carried traces of them everywhere. Hope had been a wise woman, much like Millie, with deep knowledge of folk medicine and a profound connection to nature. The air inside was still rich with the scent of dried herbs hanging from wooden beams, and every corner seemed to whisper stories of healing and wisdom.

Ruby and Anabella had grown up in this cottage, their childhood filled with the joys of life on a small farm and the enchantment of the woods that surrounded it. These woods had been Hope's sanctuary and classroom, where she communed with the spirits of the forest and learned the secrets of each plant and mushroom.

On the hill behind the cottage stood a stone cross with their names carved deeply into its base, a tribute to Jakub and Hope Jones. The cross overlooked the forest, a silent guardian watching over the land they had cherished. It was a place of reverence and memory, where Ruby and Anabella often went to feel close to their parents.

Hope's touch was evident in the cottage's every detail— from the intricately woven tapestries that adorned the walls, depicting scenes of the natural world, to the well-worn wooden shelves lined with jars of dried herbs and tinctures. Each item had a purpose, a story, and a connection to the earth and the life it nurtured.

In the pantry, a particular shelf caught Millie's attention. It was lined with jars and bottles, each filled with dried herbs and medicinal concoctions. It was a collection that exceeded Millie's own back in her village, a testament to Hope's expertise and dedication.

"Here, Millie," Ruby said, gesturing to the shelf. "These were my mother's remedies. She was a master of nature's healing powers, much like thyself. I can think of none better to inherit them." Her voice was tinged with reverence and a hint of sadness.

Millie's eyes lit up as she gently touched the glass jars, each label a whisper from the past. With a tender smile, she looked at Rufus and then back at Ruby. "Thank you, Ruby. I am honored to continue thy mother's work here," she said, her voice steady. It was her first genuine smile since the ordeal began, a sign of relief and a spark of hope that perhaps here, in this little cottage surrounded by the ancient woods, she could find peace and start anew.

Together, they continued to settle in, each object they placed, a step toward building a new life away from the shadows of the past.

A gentle rhythm of daily life had settled over the cottage by the forest as the first week passed. Millie, ever resourceful, had taken to baking bread using the bags of ground grain Patrick left for her. The oven, though aged, was reliable, and soon the aroma of freshly baked bread filled the air each morning.

The nearby neighbors, who had kindly tended to Hope's livestock after her passing, returned them to Millie. They began to trade with Millie. In exchange for her hearty loaves, they offered chickens, and eventually, Millie found herself tending to a cow and a goat as well.

Rufus, ever the helper, busied himself with chores around the property. He chopped wood for the fire that warmed their evenings and mended the pens that housed their growing number of animals. As the days passed, the semblance of a peaceful life was forming, with each task bringing them closer to the ordinary joy they had longed for.

Despite the calm, or perhaps because of it, Rufus felt the familiar pull of his nomadic spirit stirring within him. He began to speak of moving on, of returning to his teachings and the broader world beyond the cottage. Yet, before he could decide on a departure date, an unexpected visitor arrived.

Angel of the Dark Ages

CHAPTER FOURTEEN:

ANABELLA VISITS

Nearly a week had passed in Millie's new home when a knock came at the door. Rufus opened it to find Anabella standing there, her expression a mixture of urgency and relief. Curiously, by her side, sat Purity.

"Good morrow, Rufus," Anabella greeted him warmly, though her eyes flickered uncertainly between Millie and Rufus. "I trust we do not intrude, but we bring tidings—and an unexpected request."

Rufus ushered her in with a friendly nod. "Of course, Anabella. How may we be of service? Pray, enter and make yourself comfortable. What matter brings you here this day?"

Settling into a chair that Rufus offered, Anabella took a deep breath before she began. "The archbishop is gravely ill," she started, her voice tinged with a mix of worry and disbelief.

"It seems Purity here," she gestured to the cat, "bit him on the hand not long ago. Remarkably, he doesn't hold any resentment toward Purity. He confesses the bite was well deserved and has served as a kind of awakening for him. The bite is now inflamed and seeping fluids. Despite various treatments— bloodletting and the application of numerous herbs and minerals—his condition worsens. He is now convinced that only Millie can heal him."

Millie sat motionless, her eyes wide in surprise, her jaw clenched as she inhaled deeply.

Turning to Millie with earnest eyes, Anabella continued, "He has undergone a profound change, Millie. He bade me convey his deepest apologies and begs your forgiveness for his past actions. He tells me he recalls the original reasons he joined the church and now sees how far he has strayed from those noble ideals. Now, he pleads for you to save his life, as you have done for so many others."

The room fell silent, the weight of her words hanging heavily in the air. Millie sat, stunned into silence, grappling with a tumult of emotions. Beside her, Friar Rufus's expression mirrored her shock, his mouth agape, his eyes searching Millie's face for signs of her reaction.

Minutes ticked by in silence, filled only by the soft rustling of leaves outside and the heavy breathing of those in the room. Millie's hands trembled as she considered the gravity of the request from a man who only days ago sought to end her life.

At last, Millie found her voice. "How grievous is his condition? Do I even have time to return and make a difference?"

"He draweth near to death," Anabella replied solemnly. "But thou needst not travel far to see him. He awaiteth right outside in the carriage, hoping thou wilt speak to him."

Cypress, Angel, and Purity, sat together in a quiet huddle. Angel looked to Purity and asked, "Do you believe his intentions are true?"

Purity responded with a weary sigh. "I've been by his side all my life. I observed him change into something unrecognizable because of ambition and corruption. When I bit him, it was out of desperate hope to make him realize what he'd become. Instead of punishing me, he showed understanding and forgiveness. Humans often use illness as an agent of change. And so it was with him. There's a significant change in his aura now. Look for yourselves."

With a deep breath, Millie stood up resolutely. "Come, Cypress," she said, determination firming her voice as she headed toward the door. "Let us see what truth awaiteth us outside."

Cypress trailing behind, Millie stepped out into the soft light of the morning, her heart heavy yet open, ready to confront the past and perhaps, in doing so, reshape the future. As they approached the carriage, the figure of the archbishop loomed, a shadow of his former self, awaiting the mercy of the woman he once condemned.

Millie gazed at the archbishop; her face tight with controlled emotion. Holding Cypress close, she whispered softly, "Cypress, thou hast guided me through the mysteries of healing and truth for many a year. Now, gaze upon this man and tell me. What dost thou see?"

Cypress studied the archbishop intently. Gifted with the ability to perceive the true essence of beings, she scrutinized past the physical ailment that ravaged him to his core. There, she found not the hardened leader of the church but the pure colors of the earnest young man who once sought to serve with compassion and humility. With a gentle meow, Cypress hopped from Millie's arms, circled twice, and sat down—a clear signal in their shared language that the man before them was worthy of help. Millie's expression softened.

"Bring him within," she commanded. "Let us see what may be done."

Friar Rufus and Anabella carefully supported the frail archbishop, guiding him into the cottage and laying him on the bed. Millie and Cypress began their work in earnest. They sorted through herbs and potions—some familiar to Millie, others less so. Working in unison, they selected those that resonated with healing energies, each ingredient chosen for its potential to harmonize with the archbishop's ailments.

As evening approached, a sudden look of distress crossed Cypress's face. Millie noticed immediately.

"What dost we need, Cypress?" she inquired urgently.

The cat walked to the door and looked back, signaling for Millie to follow. Friar Rufus quickly lit a lantern.

"Shall I accompany thee, Millie?" he offered. "The night draws nigh."

"Thank thee, good friar. Thy company would be most welcome," she responded, following Cypress out into the twilight.

The group entered the dense woods behind the cottage with the cat as their guide. The underbrush thickened, and the forest seemed to close in around them with an almost sentient watchfulness. Cypress halted and sat down abruptly by a small, nondescript plant, barely visible in the lantern's glow.

"What is it, Cypress?" Angel asked. She and Purity had followed her.

"It's the forest spirits," Cypress said, her eyes wide as she scanned the darkening woods. "They communicate with me, guiding me to what we need. This plant here—it's important."

Friar Rufus knelt beside her. "Is this what thou need, Cypress?" he asked. Cypress began digging at the plant. Rufus got the hint and dug carefully. The task proved challenging; the root was deep and stubbornly entwined with the earth.

As Rufus labored, a small, shimmering light emerged from the disturbed soil and floated gracefully toward Millie. She was startled at first, but her eyes soon widened with recognition, and a warm smile spread across her face. She knew this gentle presence: a spirit of the forest, a guardian of the woodland secrets.

The spirit hovered near, its light dancing mere inches from her face. In the quiet of the forest, a silent exchange passed between them—a greeting, an acknowledgment of her arrival to her new family in the woods.

After several strenuous minutes, Rufus finally freed the plant, leaving its large root intact. He stood, brushing the dirt from his hands, and held up the root with a triumphant grin. "Got it," he declared.

With the precious root in hand, they returned to the cottage. Millie immediately set to work, preparing a poultice. She applied it to the archbishop's swollen hand. Then, with the cats by her side, she kept watch through the night, providing nourishment and changing his bandage with a fresh poultice every hour.

By morning, the archbishop's condition had markedly improved. He was resting comfortably, the infection receding under the persistent care of Millie's herbal knowledge.

"That is all I can do," she declared as dawn broke.

Throughout the next day, the archbishop rested, occasionally sipping the soup they offered. By the following morning, he was strong enough to sit up. Looking earnestly at Millie, he expressed his gratitude.

"I thank thee, good Millie. I owe thee my very life."

Ever the gracious healer, Millie nodded and suggested he eat something. However, the archbishop continued, his voice earnest.

"Millie, I must beseech thy pardon. I humbly ask for thy forgiveness for all I have wrought upon thee. Wilt thou consider journeying back to London with me?"

Millie paused, her eyes reflecting the weight of his request. "I shall need time to ponder upon that," she replied thoughtfully, her mind full of past grievances and a cautious hope for redemption. The room was silent as each pondered the fragile thread of reconciliation now spun between them.

"Indeed, you'll need at least another day's rest before considering travel," Millie told the archbishop.

Throughout the day, the archbishop continued to rest, gradually regaining some strength. The following midmorning, Ruby stopped by to see how everyone was faring. To her astonishment, she found not only her sister Anabella in attendance but also the archbishop, whose presence initially shocked and unsettled her. It took a moment for Anabella and Millie to detail the recent events and the archbishop's astonishing turnaround.

Ruby absorbed the news with a thoughtful expression. After some contemplation, she suggested that she and Millie take a stroll outside.

"Dear Millie, while I understand thy desire to return to thy former life, please know thou art always welcome here.

Thou mayest stay as long as thou wishest, even for the remainder of thy days if it pleaseth thee. News of thy presence hath begun to spread; many in need of healing are like to seek thee out."

"Thank thee, Ruby," Millie responded, her mind swirling with thoughts. "Tell me, hast thou ever noticed anything…unusual in the woods behind the cottage?"

Ruby chuckled softly. "Dost thou mean the sprites? That's what we have always called them."

Millie nodded, relieved. "So, I am not imagining things, then?"

"Not at all. And I am not surprised they have revealed themselves to thee. I cannot say exactly what they are, but they have always been kind and incredibly helpful, especially with healing matters. My mother—God rest her soul—used to say they are part of this world's essence. She called them elementals—a curious term, but it seems to fit. They oft communicated with her, and she dearly loved their company."

"I understand now," Millie mused, a sense of peace settling over her. "I felt an instant connection with them too."

Ruby smiled, hopeful. "Doth this mean thou wilt stay?"

"Yes, I believe I shall," Millie confirmed with a soft smile. "This place is much more peaceful, and the presence of the sprites is comforting. I need to return to mine old home for a few days to gather my belongings and settle affairs, but I will come back hither. This feels like where I am meant to be."

After their contemplative walk, Millie and Ruby made their way back to the cottage. Millie, feeling a newfound sense of resolve, approached the archbishop's bedside, where he lay recovering. She sat beside him, her expression serene but firm.

"Archbishop Gilebertus, I have made my decision regarding thy request for me to return to the township. I have been graciously offered this fair cottage to dwell in for the rest of my days. I have grown to love it here, and it is here that I intend to remain."

Archbishop Gilebertus, looking much improved but still frail, nodded slowly. "I understand, Millie. May I offer thee transport to fetch thy belongings? Perchance, during our journey, we might further discuss thy decision. I might yet persuade thee to reconsider," he proposed hopefully.

Millie smiled gently. "Thou shalt not change my mind, Gilebertus. When I first beheld this cottage and felt the peace herein, I knew it was where I belonged."

CHAPTER FIFTEEN:

MILLIE RETURNS

With arrangements made, Millie journeyed back to the township north of London with the archbishop and Friar Rufus. The ride was long, giving them ample time to converse. Despite the archbishop's attempts to sway her, Millie's resolve remained unshaken. She spoke warmly of her new life, the connections she'd made, and the sense of purpose she felt at the cottage.

"Very well, Millie, I honor thy decision as final. May I offer thee the services of a wagon to transport thy belongings back to thy cottage? Yet, I would ask a boon in return," conceded the archbishop.

"And what would that be, Archbishop?"

"Please attend mass this Sunday, as thou hast always done."

"Very well. I shall be there, as always."

"And what of thee, good friar?" asked Gilebertus. "What plans hast thou?"

"I wish to return to the Franciscan friary. I do at times teach theology at the university there, and I have much to share and discuss with mine students."

"Ah yes, I know it well. May I presume that I might be featured in these discussions?"

"Perchance thou shalt be mentioned. Wouldst thou find it grievous?"

"No matter what I may feel, the truth remaineth the truth."

News of Millie's return spread rapidly throughout the village, sparking a wave of excitement and curiosity. Her days quickly became a whirlwind of visits from neighbors and friends, all eager to see her and express their heartfelt emotions. Villagers flocked to her cottage, bringing tokens of gratitude and sorrow for her impending departure, which was planned to follow Sunday's mass.

Mothers and fathers, whose ailments had been soothed by her skillful hands, came bearing homemade goods and produce; their voices choked with emotion as they recounted the ways Millie had touched their lives.

Amidst the bustling atmosphere, conversations often turned to the harrowing events of several weeks past, when Millie and Friar Rufus had narrowly escaped the flames of persecution. Tales of that dreadful night were recounted with fervor, each villager sharing their perspective, their fear, and their relief at the narrow escape. Eyes filled with tears and voices quivered as they spoke of the terror that had gripped their hearts, and the bravery that had ultimately saved their beloved healer.

Millie listened to these accounts with a mixture of gratitude and sadness. The outpouring of love and support touched her, but the impending reality of her departure cast a shadow over her heart. The community's gratitude was palpable, yet so was their sorrow.

As the days passed, the discussions grew more poignant. Plans for Millie's journey were meticulously discussed, ensuring her safe passage to her new home. Advice was given and promises of letters and visits were exchanged. The villagers spoke of the future with hope, vowing to protect one another and honor Millie's legacy of care and compassion.

In the quiet moments between visits, Millie found herself reflecting on the bond she shared with these people. She had healed their bodies, but they had healed her spirit, giving her strength and purpose. The village had been her home, and in her heart, it always would be.

As the final day of her stay approached, the excitement and sorrow intertwined, creating a tapestry of emotions that enveloped Millie and her community. The night before her departure, a gathering was held in her honor, a time to celebrate the healer who had touched so many lives. She had been their guardian, their friend, and their inspiration.

Millie stood before them, her heart full. "I shall carry each of you with me, always," she said, her voice steady despite the tears in her eyes. "Though I must leave, my spirit remains here in this village that I love. Thank you for your kindness, your courage, and your unwavering support. I am blessed to have known you all."

As she had vowed, Millie answered the call to church on Sunday and seated herself in her favorite pew, a familiar and comforting place. The morning light filtered through the stained-glass windows, casting colorful patterns on the floor as the congregation gathered. The service began with a hymn, voices rising in unison, followed by the sign of the cross. It was then that Archbishop Gilebertus himself approached the pulpit, his presence commanding the attention of all.

"Dear devotees," he began, his voice resonant and clear, "I wish to announce that this will be the last mass over which I preside."

A loud collective gasp echoed through the church, whispers of disbelief and surprise rippling among the parishioners.

"First, it is my duty to return something which belongs to our beloved Millie." With a solemn expression, he descended from the pulpit and walked down the aisle toward Millie. The congregation watched in hushed anticipation.

Millie felt her pulse quicken as the archbishop approached her pew. She noticed Constable Luca standing and handing something to the archbishop. He nodded his thanks, then turned and walked over to her.

"Lady Millie," he said, his voice softer yet laden with earnestness, "I would return unto thee thy rosary, which I did take from thee so callously. Constable Luca and I did our utmost to remake it. I trust thou shalt find it in proper order."

Millie's face lit up with a mixture of joy and astonishment. "Oh! My rosary!" she exclaimed, clutching the beads to her heart. Overwhelmed by emotion, she wept with happiness, the familiar feel of her own beads bringing her joy and comfort.

Archbishop Gilebertus returned to the pulpit, his steps deliberate and measured. "Verily, I am departing from the holy church," he proclaimed, the gravity of his words casting a hush over the assembly. "Friar Rufus hath made provision for my entry into the Franciscan friary, where I shall take the holy vows to become a brother."

The congregation watched quietly as he spoke. His voice, usually so authoritative, now held a note of humility and resolution.

"I have strayed from the path of righteousness, and it is time for me to seek forgiveness and redemption. In the quietude of the friary, I hope to find solace and a renewed purpose. There, perchance, thou mayst seek me out."

With those words, he turned, removed the mitre, the symbol of his rank in the church, from his head, and walked away from the pulpit. The assembly sat quietly as another priest stepped forward to complete the mass, his voice steadying the congregation as he led them through the final prayers.

When the mass was completed, the congregation slowly made their way to the courtyard, where they gathered to bid farewell to Millie. The air was filled with a mix of sadness and hope, the weight of recent events heavy on everyone's minds. The sun cast a warm glow over the cobblestones, creating an atmosphere of bittersweet departure.

Standing beside Millie's wagon, Friar Rufus and Mr. Gilebertus, now a former archbishop, awaited their turn to bid farewell. Their presence drew curious and sympathetic glances from the townsfolk.

The courtyard buzzed with whispered conversations and soft farewells. Neighbors and friends approached Millie one by one, expressing their gratitude for her healing touch and their sorrow at her departure. Children who had once been healed by her gentle hands clung to their mothers' skirts, casting shy, tearful glances at the woman who had saved them.

Friar Rufus, ever the steadfast companion, stood by Millie's side, offering her quiet words of encouragement. His hand rested reassuringly on her shoulder as they shared a moment of silent understanding. Both knew the road ahead would be fraught with challenges, but they faced it with a shared determination.

Mr. Gilebertus humbly stepped forward. His eyes met Millie's with a mixture of remorse and respect. "Mistress Millie," he said, his voice soft yet earnest, "I wish thee well on thy journey. May thy path be blessed, and may thou find peace and safety in thy new home."

Millie nodded, her eyes shining with unshed tears. "Thank you, kind sir," she replied. "May thy own journey bring thee the redemption thou seekest."

As the final farewells were exchanged, Millie climbed into the wagon, her heart heavy yet hopeful. The journey to the secluded cottage awaited, promising a new beginning away from the shadows of her persecution. Friar Rufus joined her, and with a gentle flick of the reins, they began their journey.

The wagon rolled away, the figures of her former home growing smaller in the distance. Among them, the former archbishop stood quietly and watched them go.

As the wagon disappeared from view, the people slowly dispersed, each carrying a piece of the day's profound events in their hearts. The courtyard, now quiet, bore witness to the end of one chapter and the hopeful beginning of another.

CHAPTER SIXTEEN:

ANGEL'S RETURN

Millie's return to her beloved new home at the edge of the forest was swift, despite the turmoil that had once engulfed the township north of London. Within a fortnight, she settled back into the rhythm of rural life. Each morning, she walked through the dewy fields, her heart swelling with gratitude for the unexpected turn her life had taken.

Visitors from both her former township and the local village began to arrive, seeking her remedies and advice. With her deep knowledge of herbal medicine and occasional guidance from Cypress, Millie helped each one. The archbishop's visit soon faded into a distant memory, serving as a poignant reminder of her journey—from persecution to sanctuary—guided by her feline companions and the enigmatic sprites of the forest.

Cypress and Angel had become inseparable companions, each learning from the other's unique experiences and skills. Angel, ever vigilant and wise in the ways of survival, shared her knowledge of the forest's hidden dangers with Cypress, teaching her how to sense the presence of predators. In turn, Cypress imparted to Angel the ancient healing knowledge she had acquired from Millie, blending their skills to create a formidable duo.

One evening, as they sat under the expansive canopy of the forest, Angel confided in Cypress, "I cherish Millie and the love she gives, but something feels amiss."

"The Great Cat promised to return you to your time when our mission here was complete. Is that your wish, Angel? Do you desire to return to your time, to be with your human, April?"

"Yes. But I am afraid. What life will I be returning to? My brother remains here with Patrick. Will I continue to live a feral life alone?" Angel's eyes filled with a wistful longing. "More than anything, I wish to be with April. But I worry about her mother's allergy to cats. What can be done about that?"

"Let us seek guidance from the Great Cat," proposed Cypress.

That night, under a moonlit sky, Cypress and Angel convened in a secluded clearing. Tiny forest sprites, their glow illuminating the surroundings, added to the otherworldly ambiance of the night. Cypress and Angel, their eyes reflecting the moon's brilliance, stood poised in anticipation.

The air vibrated as the pulse of the forest created a magical hum. Angel whispered a silent prayer to the ancient spirits of the forest, asking for guidance and clarity from her source, a right afforded to all beings.

Suddenly, the very fabric of reality seemed to shimmer and shift. The air before them rippled, and a portal formed, glowing with an otherworldly light, finally fully materializing in the center of the clearing. The portal's glow intensified, heralding the arrival of the Great Cat.

The Great Cat emerged, its form both majestic and ethereal, exuding an aura of warmth and authority. Its eyes, deep pools of ancient wisdom, locked onto Angel.

"You have done well, Angel," the Great Cat intoned, its voice resonating with warmth and authority. "Your actions have catalyzed significant changes. You have shown the world that even the smallest and seemingly most insignificant among us can create ripples of change that spread far and wide. Your courage in the face of danger has inspired others to stand up for what is right. The miraculous events that all witnessed have shaken their convictions. It is because of you, Angel, that Millie's healing touch will restore many. The archbishop, realigned with his original purpose, will guide others toward compassion and understanding. The fabric of time has been mended and reshaped by your courage. You have brought light to the darkness. Your acts of courage and cleverness have played a small but crucial role in advancing humanity's pursuit of compassion and understanding, marking a significant milestone in their collective journey. This is the highest reason for us to exist in this form. The creator foresaw the value of this partnership, realizing that through their connection with humans, cats would help cultivate a world enriched with compassion, love and mutual respect.

The Great Cat smiled. "Go forth, Angel. Your journey does not end here. Continue to be a force for good in the world and know that you carry the spirit of the Great Cat within you."

Her heart buoyed by these words, Angel voiced her deepest wish, "I am thankful for having served a noble purpose here. Now, I yearn to return to my time, to be with April. But will I continue as a feral being, or can I be her beloved pet as intended?"

The Great Cat's gaze softened, a smile playing across its mystical features. "Angel, your devotion and bravery have not gone unnoticed. The bond you share with April is profound, spanning across lifetimes. The condition that kept you apart from April no longer holds. Skittish's decision to remain in this time has dissolved the necessity for the allergy. You were once feral out of necessity, a guardian unseen. But now, the time has come for a new role. Your wish shall be granted. You will return to April not as a feral outsider, but as her cherished companion. The path is clear, and the love you share will be the bridge that reunites you. The knowledge of this change has not yet reached her. You must be the bearer of this good news."

Angel's spirit lifted. "I believe I can do that," she said, her voice tinged with resolve and hope. "I wish to return. I'm ready to embrace my original destiny with April."

"So be it," declared the Great Cat. "Your wish is granted."

"Thank you, Great Cat," Angel said with gratitude and determination. "I am ready to embrace my destiny and return to April."

With a swirl of celestial light and a chorus of musical whispers from the forest sprites, Angel was enveloped in the warm embrace of the portal. She took a deep breath, ready to face her future, to reunite with April, and to start anew, her heart full of stories and love from a time long past yet vividly remembered.

As Angel's form disappeared into the portal, Cypress watched with a mixture of pride and melancholy. The clearing, returning to its natural state, seemed quieter, yet filled with a sense of accomplishment. Their task complete, the forest sprites dimmed their glow and retreated into the shadows.

Cypress stood alone for a moment, feeling the enormity of what had just transpired. The night was still, the forest holding its breath, as if honoring the bravery and dedication of the little cat who had changed the course of destiny. With a final, respectful nod to the spot where the portal had been, Cypress turned and made her way back through the forest, her steps light and purposeful, ready to continue her own journey.

CHAPTER SEVENTEEN:

A CURSE BROKEN

Back in her familiar surroundings, Angel stood at the threshold of April's home. The surreal journey through time had left an indelible mark on her, transforming her from a cautious feral cat into a confident, loving companion. This transformation was evident the moment April spotted her.

April was overjoyed to see her beloved cat return. The bond they had formed was now unbreakable, enriched by Angel's temporal escapades. Unlike before, when her feral instincts kept her at bay, Angel leaped into April's arms, purring loudly, showering her with affection in a way she had never done before. Angel's return was not just a reunion; it was a rebirth of their friendship.

April squealed with delight. "Angel! What's come over you? You have never been so friendly! I can hug you now!"

April and Angel spent a long time together playing and exchanging their affection.

"How about some food, Angel?" said April. She prepared to fetch the cat food that had remained untouched for weeks.

Bursting into the house, April couldn't contain her excitement. "Mom! Mom! Angel's back!" she called out, her joy bouncing off the walls. She enveloped her mother in a tight hug, filled with happiness. "She's different, Mom! She hugged me and didn't want to let go! It's like a miracle!"

Diana, her mother, was initially thrilled, but then a wave of concern washed over her. "April, you're covered in cat hair...You know how allergic I am. I might need to go to the hospital," she said, worried.

She rushed to the pantry in search of her allergy medication, her anxiety mounting with each passing second. "Where are they? Where are they?" she muttered frantically, her hands shaking in fear as she searched through bottles and boxes.

After several tense minutes without finding her pills, Diana realized something astonishing. "I'm not sneezing...There's no rash. I should be miserable right now, but I'm not. I feel fine. How can this be?" she pondered aloud, confusion and relief mingling in her expression.

Outside, Angel watched quietly through the glass door, her eyes following every movement inside the house.

"Mom, maybe you're not allergic anymore?" April suggested hopefully.

Taking a deep breath, Diana paused to consider this new possibility. With cautious optimism, she stepped closer to Angel, who was still by the door. As she opened the door, Angel greeted her with affectionate rubs and soft meows. Tentatively, Diana reached down, her hand trembling slightly as she touched Angel for the first time, still fearing an allergic reaction. Nothing happened. No sneezing, no itching, no rash. Emotions welled up inside her as she lifted Angel into her arms, feeling the warm fur against her cheek.

For Diana, holding Angel was a revelation—a moment of pure joy she had long thought impossible. She handed Angel back to April, a broad smile spreading across her face. "Looks like we've got ourselves a cat, April. I guess miracles do happen."

As they all settled into this new chapter, their dogs adapted quickly to Angel's presence. Their home filled with newfound laughter and love. Angel purred contentedly; her mission fulfilled not just in saving Millie but in bringing together a family that had once feared they could never embrace her fully. The simple joy of a cat's purr had bridged worlds and healed hearts.

THE END

Printed in Great Britain
by Amazon